THE NIGHTMARE AT MANHATTAN BEACH

A THOMAS AUSTIN CRIME THRILLER
BOOK 7

D.D. BLACK

A Note on Setting

While many locations in this book are true to life, some details of the settings have been changed.

Only one character in these pages exists in the real world: Thomas Austin's corgi, *Run*. Her personality mirrors that of my own corgi, Pearl. Any other resemblances between characters in this book and actual people is purely coincidental. In other words, I made them all up.

Thanks for reading,

D.D. Black

Life being what it is, one dreams of revenge.
- Paul Gauguin

A man that studieth revenge keeps his own wounds green.
- Francis Bacon

He who pursues revenge should dig two graves—one of them for himself.
- Old proverb

PART 1

SHADOWS OF HOME

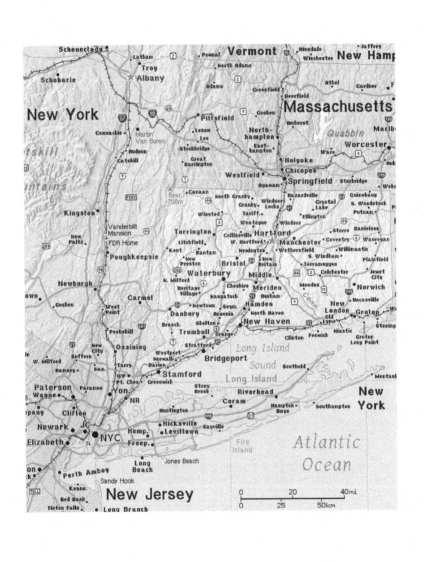

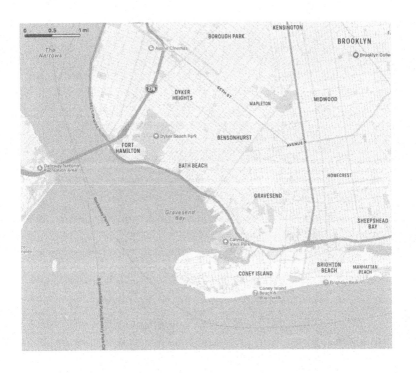

CHAPTER ONE

Manhattan Beach, Brooklyn

"HEY CARLOS, look at those businessmen playing tag," Aurelio said.

Disappointed that his brother didn't look up from his screen, Aurelio dug his toes into the sand. He continued watching through squinted eyes as the two men ran down the beach. They were wearing dark pants and fancy-looking jackets. Suits like the ones daddy wore five days a week when he took the train from their Brooklyn apartment into Manhattan to make money. The man who was "It" was about twenty feet behind the one who was running away, but neither of them looked to be having any fun.

As usual, Aurelio's older brother Carlos wasn't paying any attention to him. Instead, he was immersed in the game he'd recently downloaded onto his Nintendo Switch: *Viking Battles 3*. In the game, you sailed around the seas looking for treasure and battling sea monsters and anyone else who got in your way. And you got to drink mead and say "SKOLL" a lot, which was awesome.

Aurelio created a little boy character named "Golden Soul

the Enchanted," but Carlos had deleted it while he was sleeping. Carlos was a berserker character. In the game and real life, too.

Even though Aurelio had only gotten to play it a few times, he already considered *Viking Battles 3* the coolest game ever. And not just because he'd heard his older brother say the same.

The men, who had started far down the beach near a big wooden warehouse, were now coming in their direction, though they were closer to the water. Aurelio loved tag and he promised himself that when he was older he'd still wear shorts and t-shirts when he played. He'd never play tag in a suit.

Dad was only a short distance away—pacing next to a park bench a few feet from the sand—and Aurelio could hear him shouting money stuff into the phone: stocks, bonds, and something called 'derivatives,' which made Aurelio think of math for some reason. Dad had only taken them to Manhattan Beach once before. That time he'd been on his phone most of the time, and this time he'd taken a call within five minutes of their arrival. Still, mom said dad had to work on weekends sometimes because he had a very important job.

Aurelio tried looking at the screen of Carlos's Switch, but his brother snarled and angled it away, using his body as a shield. It was supposed to be *their* Nintendo Switch, but Carlos treated it like it was *his*.

Aurelio thought of something. "I heard that *Viking Battles 3* has a glitch where you can get infinite lives," he said, excited to know something about the game that Carlos didn't. "Saw about it on YouTube."

Carlos sighed. "*Everyone* knows about that glitch. It's like two weeks old. Quiet, FEEF-uhl, I just got to the *Cave of Eternal Treasures*."

"What?" Aurelio didn't know what feef-uhl meant, but he suspected it wasn't something nice. Again he tried to see the screen, but Carlos turned away.

He hated being the *little* brother. Carlos always got to

control the Switch and seemed to know everything about everything. Aurelio was almost six and that made him *over halfway* to ten which meant he knew a few things, too.

He stood and walked a few paces down the beach. He kicked the sand. In the few times he'd played, he'd never even gotten to the Land of Urothea.

"Dad said stay on the steps!" Carlos barked, not looking up from the game.

Aurelio ignored him and glanced at his dad, who was walking tiny laps around the bench and looking worried. Or maybe angry. He had the kind of look in his eye that meant he was doing important money stuff.

The two men chased each other until they were even with Carlos and Aurelio on the beach, though now they were on the wet sand very close to the water.

Aurelio shoved his hands in the pockets of his swim shorts. "Why…" He wanted to ask Carlos again why two grown men would be playing tag in dark brown pants and jackets, but then he had another thought.

Maybe they *weren't* playing tag.

No, they definitely weren't. The second man was trying to catch the first because they were fighting. "Carlos, I think they're fighting."

The man in front had short black hair on his head and face and, just after passing them, he angled up the beach toward the steps and the road. In his mind, Aurelio started thinking of him as *Black Hair the Fearful*. The other man—the one who was "It" if they had been playing tag—was a little larger, with long flowing blond hair kind of like Aurelio's mom. He was missing one shoe, his round face was red and sweaty and—now that Aurelio could see it—*angry*. Aurelio began thinking of him as *Red Face the Conqueror*.

"Carlos?"

His brother didn't answer.

Aurelio looked for his father, who was now a little further away, shouting something about ROI and buyouts and leveraging capital without diluting shares and tanking the stock price. To Aurelio, it all sounded like made up stuff. And not fun made up stuff like in *Viking Battles 3*.

Black Hair the Fearful reached the stairs and bounded up the first two, but tripped on the third, allowing Red Face the Conqueror to catch up. Red Face lunged for Black Hair, but missed as Black Hair rolled to the side. Aurelio heard Black Hair shout one of the bad words his dad often yelled into the phone. Something that Mom would scold him for saying, which didn't seem fair.

Red Face adjusted and jumped on top of Black Hair. For a second he thought the men might start wrestling, like Uthar and Moki did in *Viking Battles 3* after slaying the Golden Kraken.

But then the men started punching each other.

Aurelio got scared.

They really were fighting!

Red Face punched Black Hair right in the face.

Black Hair started bleeding from his nose. It was worse than the fights in the video game. Aurelio wanted to yell "Stop!" but he didn't. No one listened to six-year-olds anyway.

They tussled again, but Red Face fell and Black Hair leapt up, blood streaming down his face, and ran toward a row of houses and businesses along the road.

"Carlos, look." Aurelio said, but not loud enough for his brother to hear. Without even thinking about it, he'd wandered up the steps toward the men, away from his brother.

Aurelio's feet kept following the men. But when they crossed the road, he didn't. He wasn't allowed. He stopped under a tree and watched as Black Hair skidded to a stop in front of a white truck. He began fumbling from pocket to pocket, probably looking for his keys.

He was too late.

Red Face reached him and grabbed his neck, then pushed him toward one of the buildings, which looked to be an old house with a pizzeria on the bottom floor.

Aurelio knew that when people died in real life, they didn't drop all the treasure and weapons they'd accumulated throughout the game, but he didn't know what *did* happen. He looked both ways, then ran across the street, staying far away from the men but unable to contain his curiosity.

Aurelio heard people screaming inside the building. He heard chairs crashing. It sounded like Uthar was using his giant crystal hammer to destroy the place like he destroyed the village in Folendale. Must be Berserkers, he thought. Just like Carlos.

Aurelio's heart was beating fast as he inched closer to the window. He wished the men would stop fighting. He stood on his tip-toes and peeked in. Red Face had Black Hair in a head-lock, dragging him through an open doorway and around a corner.

Everything had gone quiet. Aurelio could no longer see anything.

He glanced back in the direction of his family. Carlos's face was still glued to the screen. His dad hadn't even noticed that he'd crossed the street. He couldn't hear his dad's words, but saw his mouth moving angrily.

Then he heard an electric buzzing sound from inside the building.

And a scream that was worse than anything he'd heard in any video game.

CHAPTER TWO

"DAMN!" Thomas Austin tossed his cellphone on the bed and looked around his cheap, barren hotel room.

The place had a double bed, a threadbare carpet, and a nightstand with a busted alarm clock and a small lamp topped with a lampshade gashed down the side like it had been in a knife fight. The one small, dirty window was covered by a frayed, mustard-colored curtain.

He'd been in Brooklyn for three days now, and after hitting dead end after dead end in his investigation, he was running out of leads.

Through his investigative efforts he'd come up with four names. The first three were Christopher Palini, Gretchen Voohrees, and Jackson Baker. He was certain that all three were connected to the Namgung crime family and the massive conspiracy that kept them in business.

But it turned out that having names was not enough—not nearly enough.

The fourth name on his list was Jorge Diaz Lopez, a former FBI agent and the reason he'd come to Manhattan Beach, Brooklyn, in the first place. He'd found evidence that his wife had been having an affair with Jorge, but it turned out she'd been working with him to bring down the Namgungs along with the corrupt elements of the NYPD and FBI, allowing them to operate. The "evidence" of the affair had been concocted to cover their tracks.

Jorge had confirmed that the other three were involved, but hadn't been able to help beyond that. Palini was the Bureau Chief of Organized Crime Control. He used his position to control investigations into the Namgungs and steer cops away from their operations. Jackson Baker was an NYPD sergeant who did Palini's dirty work—intimidating witnesses, destroying evidence, and sometimes outright murdering those who threatened to expose the conspiracy. Gretchen Voohrees was an FBI analyst, blackmailed into manipulating data to hide the scope of the Namgung's crimes.

He'd gotten in touch with some of his old FBI contacts to dig up information on Palini, but they warned him off, saying it was too dangerous to go sniffing around. Approaching Voohrees was a dead end too—she had disappeared without a trace after being suspended six months ago. And efforts to locate Baker through his former NYPD colleagues led nowhere; no one was willing to share anything concrete and Austin feared that, like Voohrees, he might be in the wind. He was chasing men and women involved in possibly the biggest corruption case in the history of the FBI and NYPD. And whoever was running the thing had done a good job covering it up.

One of the problems he'd encountered was that all three were not only well-respected members of law enforcement, they were also respected in their communities. One old friend from the NYPD had told him of Palini: "Look, man, I don't know what to tell you. Is he corrupt? Probably. But he's not Dr. Evil sitting up in a lair. He's a regular guy—a community leader who paid for a new ballfield for the little league—who might also happen to be deeply corrupt as well. Things aren't that black and white. Haven't seen him for a month or two, but even if I had, I wouldn't risk my job by going after him."

That was the call that made Austin toss his phone on the bed. Al Capone was famous for funding soup kitchens during the Great Depression, too. Giving to charity didn't mean one wasn't also a murdering psychopath.

He needed a walk.

The elevator was being repaired, so he took the stairs down three flights and stepped out of the hotel, heading toward the beach.

As Austin meandered past rows of brick townhouses and limestone apartment buildings, he caught fleeting glimpses that reminded him of his years living in the area. Through the half-drawn blinds of a first-floor window, a woman watered a jungle of houseplants, their leaves glistening like emeralds. A few people barked into cellphones, others sat on benches reading, some hurried in and out of cars. Parents pushed pastel-colored strollers while elderly couples sauntered leisurely and store owners stood in their doorways in the morning light, taking in the day.

The neighborhood was a blend of urban vitality and coastal tranquility, much busier than the solitary calm of his little beach town of Hansville, Washington. But this little Brooklyn neighborhood was also a lot more tranquil than the chaotic, pulsing city of Manhattan across the water.

Turning a corner, he stumbled upon a small, leafy park nestled between buildings. A basketball court, its paint faded by time, was the centerpiece, alive with the laughter and playful shouts of teenagers playing a weekend pickup game. On a nearby bench, under the dappled shade of an old oak, an elderly man was engrossed in his newspaper. A frail-looking teenager walked a giant black Labrador. Or was the Labrador walking him?

Austin missed Run, his corgi. She was at home being watched by Kendall Shaw, a new detective in the Kitsap Sheriff's Department with whom he'd worked on a case that had ended only days ago. It felt like weeks. Maybe months.

That meant it felt like decades ago that he'd first understood that his wife's final piece of writing—which he'd thought was the beginning of a novel—was actually related to her death. For a year he'd sat with her typewriter in his spare room, the cryptic sentences the only piece left of what he thought was her first attempt at becoming a crime novelist.

It had read:

Michael Lee Kim strolled into the parking lot of his favorite Korean restaurant in Brooklyn at 7 PM on a Tuesday. He went to Mama Dae's once a week for their grilled steak and kimchi. He'd never lived in Korea, but the meal made him think of his grandma, who passed away when he was ten. He'd worn his lucky shirt—an authentic David Bowie shirt from The Serious Moonlight Tour— because he was meeting a date. The date, Megan, turned out to be a stand-in for the Namgung crime family, and she was there to steal his identity, then kill him.

He'd chased leads stemming from those words for over a year and now here he was, wandering through a remote section of Brooklyn with little to show for it.

He inhaled deeply, taking in the savory aroma of charred meat from someone's backyard smoker intertwined with the sweet, almost tangy hint of the ocean breeze. Between the narrow gaps of the buildings, he caught sight of the shimmering waters of the Atlantic.

"*Aaaaoooooohhhhhh.*" A low, moaning scream came from around the corner. Not a scream, exactly. More of a guttural cry of anguish.

It came again and Austin hurried toward the sound and

found it coming from a homeless man sitting next to a garbage can. He was wrapped in a thick jacket that appeared much too warm for the day. His face was like beaten, creased leather, and a little broken mandolin lay on his lap.

"Do you need any help?" Austin asked.

The man didn't look up. He was in his own world.

"Aaaaooooooohhhhhhh."

He didn't look to be injured. His eyes were closed and he seemed almost calm as he let out the sound of a pain so deep it nearly brought Austin to tears.

"That's Franklin, but we call him Franklin-stan." A woman had popped her head out of a little corner store. "Did three years in Afghanistan and, well, this is what came back. Watched his brother die, and a bunch of his friends. This is just what he does now. "

"Is there anything I can do?" Austin asked.

The woman shook her head. "Seeing people you love die too soon is a special kind of anguish."

Austin nodded, took another look at the man, then continued on.

Minutes later, Manhattan Beach came into view as he turned the corner. Three curved stone steps descended from the sidewalk to the sandy beach below. Despite the warm October morning, the beach remained quiet and peaceful. A few early risers sat on the steps facing the ocean, while a handful of others strolled along the water's edge. The beige sand appeared soft and clean, with tiny seashells dotting the beach here and there. The morning sunlight glinted off the small waves lapping at the shore and, now a block away, he could still hear Franklin's anguished cries between breaks in the waves.

His cellphone vibrated in his pocket and his excitement pinged when he recognized a Brooklyn area code. Maybe it was one of the many people he'd left messages for over the last few days.

When he answered, it was the deep voice of Jorge, the former FBI agent he'd come to Brooklyn to confront. "Did you hear?"

"Hear what?" Austin asked.

"Javi. He's dead." Jorge sounded out of breath, worried, and distracted.

"Who's Javi?" Austin asked.

"Oh, right. You don't... Someone you don't know. He was connected to the case. Three years later, they're still taking people out."

"What happened?"

"Killed yesterday, right down near the beach."

"Manhattan Beach?" Austin looked around and, for the first time, noticed police tape surrounding what appeared to be a little pizzeria on the first floor of a house. "I'm there right now. I see—"

"I know you've been looking into Palini, Voohrees, and Baker, too."

"Yeah, no luck. I—"

Jorge didn't let him finish. "Voohrees and Baker are gone."

"Disappeared?"

"More likely, gone. As in, dead."

Austin let that sink in.

"Get out of there," Jorge continued. "I mean, look into this more if you want but... I'm leaving the area for a bit."

"What? When?" Austin didn't wait for an answer. "I'm coming to see you."

"Fine, but I won't be here long. This thing has become too dangerous. I have a family to consider."

Austin began jogging back in the direction of his hotel. "Look, Jorge. Gimme twenty minutes to grab my keys and drive over there."

There was a long pause, then Jorge said, "Fine, but don't let them see you come in. Enter through the neighbor's yard, two doors down, house with a white door."

"Who's *them?*"

"Half the reporters in New York City are here. The story about Fiona a few days ago, and now Javi dead. This story is breaking wide open, and things are about to go from bad to worse."

CHAPTER THREE

AUSTIN FUMBLED for his room key as he approached the hotel, but a woman who'd been leaning against the wall stepped in front of the revolving entryway door.

"Austin? So, you *are* back!"

Austin stopped a few feet away. "Do I know you?"

The woman was in her late fifties or sixties, he thought, and wore black slacks and a white button-up shirt that looked fashionable, though Austin knew next to nothing about fashion. Her silvery-gray hair was wrapped into a crescent bun and held in place by a pencil.

"It's Patch," she said, offering up a vaguely wicked smile.

Austin stepped back. *Oh, no.*

He should have recognized her. Her hair had been fading from brown the last time he'd seen her, but her sharp cheekbones and piercing blue eyes were just the same.

"Patch" was Patricia Kellerman, a formidable presence in the New York media landscape for over four decades. When Austin was in the NYPD, her caustic wit and relentless pursuit of a story made her a feared figure at the *New York Post*. In fact, she was the reporter who'd coined the name "Holiday Baby Butcher" to describe the serial killer who'd targeted babies, one of the most notorious cases he'd ever worked.

He hadn't been a fan of Patch to begin with, but this nickname she'd coined had left her permanently on his bad side. To Austin's mind, it was gross to use the death of babies to sell papers, though he knew that Patch or any other reporter would argue that the more attention the case got, the more tips the NYPD would get, and the closer they'd get to an arrest. That's what reporters always argued.

"Still with *the Post?*" Austin asked, trying to sound neutral.

She waved a hand dismissively and put on a fake frown. "Haven't you been following my career?"

Austin said nothing.

"I've got *Patch's Corner*, my blog. I do a local crime podcast. I write freelance for some magazines on New York City politics, I—"

"*Post* finally got rid of you?"

She blinked. "I graduated to bigger and better things."

Then something struck Austin that made him step back and glance around, slowly filling with paranoia. "How did you know I was here?"

She frowned again. "You know better than to ask me that. Tell me why you've been meeting with Jorge Diaz Lopez."

Austin tried to play it cool, but inside he felt something he rarely felt: *panic*. Not only did he have nothing new about Fiona's murder, Patch seemed to know more about his activities, and location, than she had any right to.

"Here's what I'm thinking," Patch said, shoving her hands in the pockets of her elegant slacks and pacing back and forth in front of the hotel entryway, being careful not to give Austin enough of an opening to escape inside. "Dogged detective that you were—or *are?*—you've been looking into what happened to Fiona, then that article hit the *Times*, and you came here to try to break this thing?"

The article Patch was referring to had been written by Anna, whom he'd been dating until a few days ago. It had been the first big story about the case in the New York press in years.

"Instead of stalking me," Austin said, "why aren't you following up on that story, maybe trying to do some *actual* reporting?"

She sighed. "Believe it or not, speaking with you is *part* of my reporting. Care to comment on the piece?"

Austin glared at her.

"Gimme something, Austin, for old times' sake. I promise not to call you the Blue Widower of Manhattan. Again."

Austin said nothing.

She smiled. "You know, Blue, because you're a cop. Or were..."

"Christopher Palini, Gretchen Voohrees, and Jackson Baker." Austin heard the names come out of his mouth before he'd decided to share them with her.

Maybe it was because he was at a dead end. Maybe it was because he was exhausted. Or maybe it was because, despite being one of the most annoying reporters in the city for his entire NYPD tenure, she was relentless and could chase down a lead better than almost anyone.

He let out a long, thin stream of air. "All three are involved in drugs, crime, coverup. Or maybe *were*. As in, their involvement might be past tense. Their *lives* may be past tense. Directly or indirectly, all were involved in Fiona's murder, that I know for sure. You want to break a story that matters, find some proof of that and get it out there."

Austin shoved past her and hurried up to his room, closed the curtains tightly, and dropped to his knees next to the bed, then slid the gun case out from under it.

He'd followed all the TSA regulations and declared the firearm on his flight. He was supposed to get a New York permit to carry the weapon in the city, but he had no intention of doing so. He didn't have the time. Keying in the combination until the tumblers rolled smoothly into place, he opened the lid, revealing the MR1911, a classic piece of firearm engineering, nestled within. Austin curled his fingers around the pistol's cool grip, lifting it carefully from the foam. With familiar, practiced motions, he engaged the safety and removed the magazine, inspecting the gleaming .45 ACP rounds inside. He reinserted the magazine with a satisfying click and pulled back the slide, its motion smooth along the rails as it revealed the empty chamber.

Having completed his inspection, Austin re-engaged the safety and opened his concealed shoulder holster. With a final, respectful glance at the pistol, he slid it securely into place, its steel frame settling against the leather.

He didn't want to use it, but if Patch had found him, anyone could.

He no longer felt safe without it.

CHAPTER FOUR

AUSTIN PARKED his rental car a block from Jorge's house, careful to avoid drawing attention. As he approached the brownstone on the quiet Manhattan Beach street, he noticed a few reporters and a TV news van. Not half of the New York City press as Jorge had warned, but it was clear that interest in this story was increasing.

A couple doors down, there was the house with the white door. He veered off the sidewalk, keeping out of sight. Ducking between two houses, he entered a backyard, then leapt a series of low fences and crept along the edge of Jorge's fence. Shielded from view by overgrown bushes, he made his way to the side porch.

He tapped quietly on the glass door, and waited.

Maria, Jorge's wife, answered the door. She was tall, with long brown hair, and she looked none-too-pleased to see him. As she swung the door open and ushered him in, all she said was, "Jorge said you were coming."

"I'm sorry," Austin said as she closed the door behind him. "About all of this."

They entered the small, first-floor kitchen, where only days earlier he'd sat to confront Jorge about the suspected affair.

Maria stood at the fridge for a moment, then spun around and glared at him. "You *should* be sorry. You re-opened this can of worms, and now Javi is dead and—" she turned away and leaned on the sink, unable to maintain eye contact through her grief and rage. "We took my children to their grandmother's house in the Bronx two days ago. And now..."

"You *knew* Javier?" Austin asked. "The man who died?"

Without turning around, she nodded.

She turned slowly and her anger appeared now more like sadness tinged with fear. "He was one of Jorge's informants. When he was with the Bureau. Javi had done some bad things, but he'd changed and I..." she turned and pointed at the table. "I fed him here. I mean, we barbecued together on the weekends for God's sake. He would sit right here, at *my* table. He told me he liked my enchiladas better than he liked his own mother's." Her voice cracked and tears formed in her eyes.

"I'm sorry, I... I don't..." Austin didn't know what to say.

He didn't know Javi, didn't know what was going on. But it was clear that Maria blamed the man's death on the fact that Austin had shown up in New York.

"Javi told every pretty lady he liked their enchiladas better than his own mother's," Jorge said. "Dude was a grade-A liar." He'd appeared in the doorway and his comment got Maria to smile through her tears.

He waved Austin into the living room, leaving Maria alone in the kitchen.

Jorge was at least half a foot shorter than Austin, stout, with a pleasant, round face and a goatee that seemed from a different era. As he waved Austin into an armchair, he sighed and took off his thin, wire-frame glasses.

Then he tossed Austin a cellphone. "Before you watch what's on that video, I need to tell you about Javi."

Jorge put his glasses back on and walked to the window, peeking out between the drawn curtains. "When I was still with the FBI, for nearly a decade, I'd been relying on Javier Perez. He was one of my most trusted criminal informants within the Namgungs. Even though he was just a low-level runner and enforcer, Javi had this uncanny knack for moving freely within the organization, befriending both the brutal lieutenants and the street-level workers slinging product on the corners. Everybody loved him. Trusted him."

He moved away from the window and sat back down. "I flipped Javi after an assault arrest back in 2010 in Coney Island and realized fast that Javi could offer a rare glimpse into the bonds between the crooked officers in the NYPD and FBI and the Southeast Asian cartels dominating the heroin trade that flowed through the piers and warehouses along the Brooklyn waterfront. What really caught my attention was his knowledge of the cartel members and their connections within the NYPD and FBI. He knew their habits, their hangouts in Bensonhurst and Sheepshead Bay, and here, in Manhattan Beach. They've got multiple businesses here and Javi was killed yesterday in the storage room of one of their pizzerias. A little kid—six years old—is still being questioned by police. Apparently he saw it go down." Jorge shook his head in disgust. "Over the years, Javi supplied me with evidence and testimony that implicated dozens of corrupt officials."

"But never enough to convict?" Austin asked.

Jorge looked up. "We—Fiona and me—we *had* enough to convict—but then, well, you know what happened." Jorge stood, glanced toward the window nervously, then sat again. "And Fiona, I think *she* had even more. You know how it is. She and I worked together closely, but I didn't tell her everything and I'm damn sure she didn't tell me everything either. The ones we had, we both knew they weren't the top. I think she was closer to the top than me, and maybe that's why I was allowed to live."

"And Javi?"

"Well, informants are never allowed to live once they're found out." He shook his head. "Click play on that video."

Austin's grip tightened on the iPhone, the small screen glowing. He tapped to play the video and immediately recoiled. The bloody face of a man he assumed to be Javier filled the screen, then the shot zoomed out, placing Javi in a nondescript room, its walls lined with bags of flour and cans of crushed tomatoes. The room was brightly lit with harsh fluorescent lights from above, making the blood covering Javi's face almost cartoonishly red.

Javier sat cross-legged on the floor in the room's center. He was sweaty and his dark brown suit was rumpled and stained. His gaunt face was shadowed with stubble that hinted at days without care. The subtle traces of bruising along his jawline, the way he winced when he moved too quickly, hinted at physical abuse. The terror in his eyes was palpable. They darted around the room like they were chasing a ghost, indicating a psychological torment to accompany the physical one. Austin imagined his captor right off camera, likely pointing a gun at his head and possibly wielding various devices of torture.

Javier began to speak, his voice a ragged whisper, each word heavy and slow as if dragged from a well of despair. "I have done things, bad things..." He glanced up as though taking a cue from someone in the room. "Others have, too. I am... about to pay... for my loose lips with... my life." His words were jarring, filled with uneasy pauses, as if navigating a verbal minefield. "Don't make the same mistake I made."

He looked up expectantly, as though repeating the words he'd obviously been forced to say might save him from his fate.

It didn't.

For half a second, Javi locked eyes with the camera, a silent plea etched into his gaze.

The next sound Austin heard was a quick double tap. The *pop-pop* of a semi-silenced weapon.

Austin saw the blossom of crimson spread across Javi's chest as he toppled backwards. Then the video ended.

Austin and Jorge sat for over a minute, neither saying a word.

Finally, Austin said, "A reporter found me, was outside my hotel, waiting for me."

"That means they know where you are. I'm heading to Jersey. My wife's brother has a little house we're gonna stay at for a few days. You should get out of here, too. They're tying up loose ends." He stood and stepped toward Austin, staring down at him. "The article your friend Anna wrote spooked them. I don't know who, ultimately, is behind this thing. Maybe Fiona did, maybe she didn't. But what I do know is that someone is cleaning house. I don't want to end up dead. And I don't want a video of your execution sent to me and my wife."

"She watched that video, too?" Austin asked.

Jorge inhaled deeply and looked down, then out the window. "The things I've put her through."

Austin said, "I'm gonna give myself a little more time and—"

"And *what?*" Jorge interrupted. When Austin didn't continue, Jorge let out a frustrated breath. "Go back to Washington, man."

"Seventy-two hours. If I don't get anything by then I'll—"

Jorge leaned in and grabbed Austin by the shoulders. "Did you even watch that video? If you stay around here poking your nose into things, you'll be *dead* in seventy-two hours."

Maria appeared in the doorway that connected the living room to the kitchen. "Jorge, *mi amor*, it's time to go."

Jorge let go of Austin's shoulders and raised up slowly, offering Maria a sympathetic look. The kind of look a hundred men and women in law enforcement give their spouses every day. A look that said: *I'm sorry for the danger.*

It was the kind of look Austin had given Fiona on more than one occasion, both of them assuming that it was he who had the more dangerous job. They'd been wrong.

"Okay," Jorge said.

Austin stood and headed for the kitchen. "I'll sneak out the back."

Jorge followed in and stopped him before he could leave. "Austin, do you know the saying about revenge?"

Austin turned and shrugged.

"*He who pursues revenge should dig two graves—one of them for himself.* Take my advice, would you? Go home."

CHAPTER FIVE

YOU'LL BE *dead in seventy-two hours*. Jorge's words played on a loop in Austin's mind as he parked his rental car and headed for the hotel.

The neighborhood had gone quiet, a midday lull. Folks heading indoors to flee the heat, which had descended on the city streets. Combined with yesterday's rain, the heat seemed to unearth a thousand smells at once.

Half a block from the hotel he noticed a black sports car with bright silver rims. He wasn't sure if it had been there earlier, but it looked out of place in this modest neighborhood.

Austin studied the two bulky silhouettes sitting in the front seats of the idling car, his pulse quickening. Looking up at the hotel, he scanned the windows. Most of the curtains were closed, but not the mustard-colored ones of his third-floor room. They were partially open, though he was sure he'd left them closed.

Austin's neck prickled with unease.

The car's engine continued to rumble menacingly as the two men stared straight ahead. Their eyes appeared to be trained on the door of the hotel.

He stepped into a doorway—out of the line of sight of the

car—and pretended to check his phone, buying time to assess the danger. A police siren wailed in the distance, then suddenly cut off into silence. The quiet felt heavy. Ominous.

Austin's eyes darted around, evaluating possible threats, landing eventually on the partially-open curtains of what he was sure was his room.

Then he looked down.

There. Across the street.

A shadow in the alley. Was it growing, shifting, moving closer?

No, it was nothing.

Austin's breath quickened. His palms dampened.

Still pretending to make a call, he tapped his camera app and zoomed in, snapping a bunch of photos in rapid succession, hoping to catch a clear shot of the car and the license plate. Then, turning abruptly, he walked back in the direction of his rental car, keeping his pace measured and steady so as not to break into a panicked run. He resisted the urge to glance back.

Just keep walking, he told himself.

Thinking fast, he hopped back in his rental car, made a u-turn, drove around the block, and parked in between two large trucks in the parking lot of a liquor store.

"Think, Austin," he said out loud. "Think."

He tried to control his breathing, but he kept seeing the video of Javier toppling over. He believed he'd just come within a few moments of suffering the same fate.

"Think!"

How had they located him? What could he do next?

If they'd found his hotel, they might know about his rental car.

But how?

Somehow they'd tracked his flights, or cellphone, or credit card. Maybe Patch was working with them, or maybe they'd each found him independently.

It didn't matter.

For now, he needed to get away, far away.

He opened his phone and found the QuickCar App. He'd used the app a couple times in Seattle. Sometimes it was easier to take the ferry across the water and grab a car downtown. He could use it for half the day for under forty bucks and it meant he didn't have to drive his truck onto the ferry, then navigate the beast through Seattle's impossible hillscape.

Within a few taps, he'd located an available rental only six blocks away and reserved it. Eyes shooting from mirror to mirror, he eased out of the parking lot.

Reaching the QuickCar a few minutes later, he left his rental in the parking lot of a grocery store, scanned his phone on the sensor of the 2020 Toyota sedan, and got in.

He double checked his surroundings for the black sports car and, convinced he was safe, peeled out of the parking lot. He didn't know where he was going, but he had his gun, his phone, and his wallet. He knew he couldn't stay here.

His phone. More than likely, that's how they'd tracked him. Checking his rearview mirrors every few seconds, he convinced himself that he wasn't being followed, at least not yet, but he couldn't take a chance. After ten minutes he pulled into a gas station, found the restroom, and locked the door behind him.

He checked the photos he'd taken. *Damn.* He'd been too rushed, too careless. He hadn't gotten a shot of the license plate of the car parked outside his hotel.

Next he smashed his phone against the porcelain sink until it broke into bits, which he dropped in the trash. In the store, he bought two disposable cell phones, each pre-programmed with ninety minutes of call time.

Feeling a bit better, he followed signs to Route 678, doubling back and doing a few random turns to ensure that he wasn't being followed. Route 678 led him out of Brooklyn, into Queens, and across the Whitestone Bridge, which brought him to Route

95 heading towards Connecticut. The traffic was slow at points, but an hour later he'd made it onto the bridge, the gleaming skyline of Manhattan disappearing in his rearview mirror.

Stopping at a rest area, he called Kendall, who picked up after two rings. "Hello?"

"It's Austin. I had to get rid of my phone, and I'm no longer at the hotel. I, well, I had to get out of town."

After a long pause, Kendall said, "You sound like hell. Tense."

He ignored this. "How are you?"

"I'm sitting in your café eating pancakes and staring out at the water. It's bliss. I needed a break."

"How's Run?"

"She's good. She and Ralph are best friends. They learned how to play tug with each other. As you can imagine, it's adorable. By the way, speaking of dogs, remember Bjorn? I finally found him a home."

She was referring to the friendly, wild German Shepherd owned by a man they'd recently arrested. "Who's taking him?"

"Jimmy and Lucy."

"That's great." Austin *was* happy to hear it, but he had other things on his mind. He wanted to tell Kendall that, if anything happened to him, she should take care of Run. Ralph was also a corgi, so he'd trust Kendall to take good care of Run. But he didn' say it. Couldn't bring himself to say it. "Hansville treating you well?"

"Good food and coffee. Kinda odd that I came from LA not too long ago and now you're back in New York City and, by the sound of your voice, all the stress of that place has seeped right back in. I think I'll stay put. What's going on there? Are *you* doing okay?"

"Look," Austin said, "It's too hard to explain everything that's going on out here, and I'd rather not say in the first place. You can reach me on this number now, but I may go dark for a few days."

"Gotcha. Take care of yourself, okay?"

He was going to say "Okay," but he didn't want to lie to her. "Take care of Run, and give her extra treats for me and tell her I'll see her soon. Probably see her soon."

"Austin, you don't sound good. Are you sure you shouldn't just come back now?"

"Thanks for holding down the fort. Bye, Kendall."

He hung up and pressed on, crossing over into Connecticut, navigating the streets by memory. Left at the old schoolhouse, right at the tiny white church built over two hundred years ago, and then down a long driveway. He stopped his car at a large stone house and looked up at the ivy-covered facade.

He got out and stood there for a long time, just staring up at it, flooded with memories. The front door opened and a woman emerged. She wore a light blue pin-striped apron and appeared to be halfway through cooking dinner. She squinted down from the porch.

"Mary, it's me. Austin."

It was Mary, Fiona's mother, and this was the home of Fiona's parents.

"Tommy? Is that you?"

He didn't let anyone call him Tommy except for Fiona's mother.

CHAPTER SIX

AN HOUR LATER, Austin sat on the overstuffed ivory leather chair as Fiona's parents stared at him from across their large living room. They looked concerned.

He was lost in a memory of Fiona. Shortly after they were married they'd returned from their honeymoon and spent a few days with Fiona's parents. Austin recalled sitting in this very chair. It was big enough for the both of them, Fiona sitting on the armrest, legs draped over his lap. Austin felt the reality of having been robbed of the chance to be close to her like that ever again. The taste of scotch bonnet peppers tingled his throat and burned his tongue. The rage was a familiar feeling, but he hadn't felt it so strongly in a long time, not since before he moved to Washington State.

His fists had clenched into balls at his side, his body viscerally preparing for some kind of revenge. He slowly relaxed them, feeling himself sink further into the deep seat, waiting for someone to speak.

"Would you like a refill?" Sven asked, his voice raised above the sound of the TV playing quietly in the background. As he held up the bottle of wine, Fiona's father Sven looked like he belonged on the cover of *Rich Boaters Monthly* magazine: deeply tanned with a full head of blond hair so pale it had almost gone white. Tall, lean, and lithe, he wore linen shorts and deck shoes until the weather dropped below fifty degrees.

"No, but thanks," Austin said. "It's good, though."

Sven was also a wine fanatic, and had the money to buy the good stuff. Austin knew little about wine, but he could taste the difference between the two kinds of cheap wine he served in his café and whatever the deep purple nectar in the glass in his hand was.

For an hour they'd been talking around Austin's reasons for coming back to the east coast. Fiona's parents had seen the recent article about their daughter, but hadn't wanted to come right out and talk about it. And that was fine by Austin. The moment he'd stepped into their house, he'd regretted coming at all. Not because he wasn't happy to see them. He was.

He'd double-backed enough to be certain he hadn't been followed. But, even so, he didn't know what was going on and worried about involving them.

Fiona's mother sipped her wine, then accepted a refill from her husband. "How long do you think you'll stay, Tommy?" She brushed her hair off her forehead and tapped her foot against the side of the couch nervously.

"Not long," Austin said.

Sometimes Austin wondered whether Fiona would have looked like her mother when she reached her seventies. He thought so. He'd seen pictures of Mary in her thirties and forties and she looked much like Fiona had. Mary's ancestry was Swedish, Sven's Norwegian, and Fiona had inherited much of the Swedish farm girl look of her mother.

"And, remind us why you came east?" Sven asked.

Mary shot her husband an uncomfortable look. She was someone who did not enjoy confrontation or directness.

Austin looked into his wine glass, then let himself take in the details of the room, which had been redesigned since he'd last visited. Clean lines and a muted, neutral color palette lent an airy, relaxed feel to the place. Floor-to-ceiling windows overlooked the couple's sprawling backyard and allowed ample natural light to flood the space. The furniture consisted of sleek but comfortable pieces—a linen-upholstered sofa, two polished wood and leather armchairs, and an oval, glass-topped coffee table. The room was also full of nautical accents, like a ship's wheel console table, canvas photographs of sailboats, and a couple of vintage sailing regatta posters. The built-in shelves displayed trophies from decades of competitive sailing, as well as leather-bound books, a crystal decanter collection, and a few carefully chosen fine wine lithograph prints that exemplified their appreciation for finer things.

"Tommy?" Mary asked, "are you alright?"

"Not really." He met eyes with her briefly, then let his gaze fall back onto his wine glass. "I think you two have done a better job of dealing with the loss of Fiona than I have."

Mary's mouth turned into a slight frown, but she said nothing.

"We grieved," Sven said. "We still grieve." His face contorted with the word *grieve*, as though the word itself twisted an old knife lodged deep in his body. "But we have to live. We have no other choice."

Austin nodded. He knew that was true, but didn't know—had *never* known—how to move forward. Moving across the country didn't seem to have helped and returning remained inconclusive. One certainty was the longer he sat in their living room, the more he felt like he'd failed.

In an adjoining room, Fiona's brother James barked into his cellphone while his twelve-year-old daughter Olive sang along to pop songs. "How long are they here for?" Austin asked.

Mary smiled brightly. "Few more days. James' wife is at a business conference for the week, and since they homeschool anyway, they came to stay. We love spending time with Olive." She stood. "I'll head up and set up the second guest room for you."

Austin nodded. "Oh Mary, I can do that."

"Tommy, it's nothing," she insisted, and she was off in a flash.

"Son..." Sven seemed to be holding his breath. If Austin was Sven's son, that meant his daughter should be there with them. "Trust me, you'll make the bed all wrong."

They both smiled at his jest, but his glassy eyes revealed an attempt to hold back tears.

Austin had met Olive on the way in, but she hadn't taken her headphones off for more than a couple seconds. As though she could sense they'd been talking about her, Olive appeared under the large arched entry that connected the formal living room to the—Austin didn't know what it was called. Maybe a *smoking room* back in the day, but a modern realtor would likely call it a *bonus* room.

Olive stared at him as she took off her headphones, but she didn't say anything.

"What are you listening to?" Austin asked.

She rolled her eyes. "Taylor."

"Swift?" Austin asked.

She nodded cautiously. "You know her music?"

"Sure," Austin said. The truth was, he wasn't certain he'd heard many of her songs, but he wanted to connect with Olive. Like Fiona's mother, the girl resembled Fiona. Sandy blonde hair, lean, and with a pleasant face only soured by the fact that she was determined to be skeptical of everything Austin said.

Olive folded her arms and frowned. "Name your favorite Taylor Swift song." She was highly dubious.

Austin's mind raced. He was fairly sure he'd heard some of her songs, but he didn't know there was going to be a quiz. "I think, um, *Blank Space*? I've heard that one, I think." He recalled a viral video someone had shown him in which a police officer sang along with it in his cruiser.

Olive rolled her eyes even harder. "That is *sooooo* embarrassing for you."

Sven, who'd walked over to inspect a replica wooden sailboat on the mantel, chuckled, but Austin didn't understand.

Olive recognized his confusion and appeared happy to explain. "I thought you said you know her music. Um, liking *Blank Space* is like saying pizza is your favorite food but pepperoni is the only kind you've tried."

Austin shrugged. "I *like* pepperoni pizza."

"Everyone does. Pepperoni pizza is good, but there's so many other kinds! Taylor has a ton of albums and songs that are way less famous but also *way* better. You just know the one song they played on the radio like a gazillion times. If you really like her music, you should listen to the full albums she made. Like *Speak Now* or *Folklore*. They have some really good songs that weren't singles. So before you call yourself a Swiftie, maybe you should expand your horizons a little, ya think?"

She finished her rant with a sly grin, half-joking but also half-serious with her critique of his narrow musical tastes.

"I'll strongly consider it," Austin said, smiling. With the way his day had gone, this was the sort of lecture that actually made it better.

With that, Olive put her headphones back on.

"I need to make a quick call," Austin said to Sven.

Mary appeared in the doorway. "Your room is all set."

Austin sat on the bed and looked around the room. For a *second* guest room, it wasn't half bad. A king-sized bed, gleaming hardwood floors, and windows that looked toward the water, though it was too dim to see much other than the endless darkness of the ocean.

There was a picture of Fiona on the bedside table. It must have been from the visit after their honeymoon, and Austin wondered if Mary had the same memory of them sitting on the leather chair while in the living room. Maybe the picture had just been there. If she thought to place it for him, it was a sweet gesture. And Sven was right, the bed couldn't have been made more meticulously.

During the conversation with Fiona's parents Austin had been distracted by a nagging sensation that coming here had been a mistake. He didn't know how Patch had found him at the hotel, didn't know how the men at the hotel had found him, or even who they were.

But he knew someone who might be able to help.

He slid one of his burner cell phones out of his pocket and dialed Samantha, the Kitsap Sheriff Department's expert on all things technology. She'd helped him with multiple technology projects in the past and had a boyfriend whom she referred to as a "white hat hacker," a hacker who only used his skills for good. Despite the fact that Austin didn't even know his name, he'd helped out at a pivotal moment during a recent case.

He hoped they might be up for helping him again.

The only problem was that her phone was going straight to voicemail.

CHAPTER SEVEN

SAMANTHA LEANED back in her chair and kicked her bare feet up on the desk. Her phone buzzed on her lap and she silenced it without breaking eye contact with Andrea, her temporary new boss.

Andrea glanced at Samantha's bare feet as though she might object, then cocked her head and launched into one of her pep talks. "Sam, this is crisis mode, all hands on deck, pulling out all the stops. Bottom of the ninth, two outs. Fourth quarter, down by six. Choose your metaphor and run with it, right? The oppo dumps on Rid are coming in hard and fast and we need to hit back, harder."

"And faster," Byron added. Samantha hadn't even noticed him standing behind her in the doorway.

Andrea was Ridley Calvin's campaign manager, Byron her quiet, data-oriented deputy. Samantha had nothing against them, but they were acting as though the fate of the entire universe hung on this election. Samantha had never been one to follow politics, but when Ridley had asked her to do a little freelance work for his campaign, she'd said "Of course" out of loyalty to him—and trust *in* him—rather than any real attachment to the outcome of the election.

When she'd agreed to work on Ridley's gubernatorial campaign, she'd made two demands of her own. The first was that she had to finish all her official work for the Kitsap Sheriff's Department first. The second was that she wouldn't follow any dress code. If she was going to work nights and weekends for a politician—even one she respected as much as Ridley—she wasn't going to consider her attire in the least, and felt that no one else should either.

And since she wouldn't be doing anything public facing anyway, Andrea had agreed. So there she sat in jeans, a *Thor* t-shirt, and no shoes, making decisions that might swing the special election for the next Washington State governor.

Andrea moved to the doorway. "Watch that report again and then..." Andrea jabbed a thumb at Samantha's setup of two laptops on the desk... "find something we can use to hit back."

Andrea left and Byron followed wordlessly behind.

Samantha swung her feet to the floor and swiveled the chair around to face one of the laptops, concealing her laughter. She always enjoyed how people without tech backgrounds treated computers like some sort of mysterious box. The way Andrea had pointed at the laptops was like they were some dark, confusing, even magical thing. Something that could get them what they needed or ruin their day—almost as if they were sentient.

Samantha saw her computers for what they were: tools. Like a corkscrew or a chainsaw, her laptops were tools, although hers gave her access to the world's information, not wine or felled trees.

She'd already watched the latest news report once. Its airing that evening had sent Ridley's campaign headquarters into a tizzy. If she was going to dig up dirt on Ridley's opponents, she needed to be sure what kind of stuff she was looking for, so she decided to give it another watch. Kicking her feet up on the desk and admiring the new binary code tattoo on the side of her foot, she pressed play on the video.

The news anchor was the very definition of a stuffed-shirt, as generic-looking as anyone she'd ever seen. A Ken doll rip-off with a spray tan and too much product in his hair. But he read the teleprompter with gusto and, despite her skepticism, she couldn't help but be drawn in.

As the gubernatorial gladiatorial match reaches a boiling point, scandalous skeletons from Ridley Calvin's closet are being paraded for all to see. This is Chuck Ferris, bringing you the scoop on your Five O'clock Kitsap News Update.

The dirt-digging dossier that dropped today dishes up two spicy morsels from Ridley's rookie days in law enforcement. The first is a lawsuit from the nineties in which Benjamin Gardener, a suspect nabbed by Ridley for armed robbery, accused our aspiring governor of going full-throttle with the tough-guy act during his arrest.

According to Gardener, Ridley slammed his head into the side of his police car repeatedly after he'd apprehended him—after Gardener was handcuffed.

The case, however, was dismissed before reaching trial as multiple officers testified that Gardener had instigated the fight by headbutting Ridley.

The second tidbit reveals Ridley's penchant for fisticuffs during his off-duty hours. Eyewitness accounts paint a picture of a hot-headed, pugnacious young officer frequenting the local bar scene and getting into scuffles on more than one occasion.

In one instance, a man named Gregory Pentolio filed charges for assault, claiming that Ridley broke his nose in a bar fight. The case was never pursued due to "lack of evidence," according to the files.

But according to Pentolio, Calvin's buddies in law enforcement "killed the case."

These decades-old incidents never saw the light of a courtroom. But in an election teetering on a razor's edge, even a whiff of scandal could tip the scales.

The Ridley campaign has vociferously denied any wrongdoing, pegging the allegations as nothing more than desperate, eleventh-hour mudslinging. Both the Daniels and Carter campaigns have denied any involvement in the leak of this incriminating material.

In our latest poll, Ridley trails his former boss, Sheriff Grayson Daniels, by only three points, and Carter is pulling up the rear with twenty-six percent of the vote, still within striking distance, though outside the margin of error.

I'm your guide through the political maelstrom, Chuck Ferris, and with the D-Day of Election Day looming, only time will tell if these accusations stick, or if voters brush off these last-minute theatrics.

Over to you, Dana.

Samantha's phone rang again—a number she didn't recognize. The same number that had called during her chat with Andrea. "Hello?"

"Samantha, it's Austin."

"Hey there, I'm at Ridley's campaign headquarters and things are nutty right now. What's up?"

Austin sighed. "A lot is up, but first, how is Ridley, and the campaign? I admit I haven't been following it much."

"Three way tie, basically. At least that's what our polls show. News says Daniels is out front by a little. Someone just unloaded a bunch of opposition research on Ridley. It's nothing too bad, at least to me it isn't. My bet is that his opponents have a lot worse skeletons in their closets."

Austin chuckled weakly. He sounded tired. "And you're going to find them, I bet."

"That's what they're paying me for, but I know you didn't call for the latest poll numbers. What's up?"

"I flew out here using my real name. I rented a car using my real name. Later, I checked into a hotel and paid cash. Only place I could find that didn't require an ID. And yet, a *reporter* found me and, I think, someone worse than a reporter. I'm thinking they tracked my phone, maybe."

The way he said the word *reporter* made it sound like he was describing a terrorist. Samantha knew about Austin's distaste for reporters, except for a certain local reporter named Anna, with whom—at least as far as Samantha could tell—Austin had had an on-again off-again flirtation. She was going to ask him about it, but realized quickly how inappropriate that would be. "My guess is that you're calling me to ask how they found you?"

"I know there are lots of ways to track people these days."

"There are so many obvious ways they could have found you," Samantha interrupted. "You said you rented the car under your real name, with a credit card?"

"I did, but—"

"The reporter could've gotten your location by hacking your emails, impersonating you on the phone to the hotel, tracking your license plate through street cameras, using facial recognition on surveillance footage, or even just getting tipped off by someone on staff."

On Samantha's monitor, the news report was playing on repeat, pulling her attention away. She could hear the impatience in her own tone. "Look, I know you're still getting up to speed on digital footprints, but these days when you travel across the country, especially to work a high-profile case, you can pretty much assume your movements and location data are vulnerable through both legal monitoring and shady underground means. I really wish you'd been more careful to stay off the grid."

"Okay, so now I've gotten rid of my cellphone, got a temporary car, one of those QuickCar things—"

"Which is harder to track, but if they've hacked your apps..."

"But I got rid of my phone."

"They can still track data from *within* your apps. The car itself has a location tracker in it, which updates to the apps on the central servers, not just on your phone." She stood and walked a lap around her chair. "Look, Austin. It's unlikely they hacked the car company. They would have had to have known that you used that company, and these things are actually a lot harder than they look on TV. So they're probably not on you right now. But they could be, and you need to be more careful."

"I'll get rid of the car soon. If I want to stay unnoticed, what else should I do?"

Samantha sat back down. "Don't use credit cards, don't use your real name, don't tell anyone else you're there."

There was a long silence, then Austin said, "I need help."

He sounded exhausted, and less confident than she'd ever heard him. "With what?"

"I wish I knew."

CHAPTER EIGHT

AUSTIN ENDED THE CALL. He *did* need help, and he truly didn't know with what.

He heard the muffled sound of the TV coming through the floor. Fiona's father was a news junkie, and Austin had no doubt he was watching the nightly news.

He headed down to find Sven in the living room where he was indeed watching the evening news. Despite the fact that they were in Connecticut, they were close enough to New York City that they could pick up their local channels.

Sven looked up briefly and nodded as Austin sat down in the *Fiona memory* loveseat, acknowledging Austin's presence without actually having to speak.

That was fine by Austin. He felt more adrift and less committed than he ever had before. He'd read a book once in which someone described returning to their childhood home and "regressing"—losing their adult faculties and essentially becoming a child again, in mind and spirit, though not in body.

And although this wasn't *his* childhood home, he wondered whether that might be happening. He'd never been fully comfortable here. Fiona's parents had always been welcoming, of course, but he wasn't comfortable with their wealth, their formality.

And with Fiona gone, the person who'd tied them together, who'd made them into a family, he didn't feel that thread of connection he'd always felt.

So he stared at the TV, sitting across from Sven in silence.

After a brief segment on a new initiative to reduce homelessness in the city and an on-scene report from a big security conference that both the New York and Connecticut governors were attending, the news cut to a somber-faced anchor.

"And now some disturbing news from just across the bridge in New Jersey," the man began. "A brazen daylight abduction of a former FBI agent has left his wife and children in tears and law enforcement racing for answers. Myra, fill us in on the latest..."

The shot changed to a young reporter with long black hair. She wore a red blazer and was standing next to...

Oh no, that was Maria, Jorge's wife.

"Please," the reporter said, "tell us what happened." She angled the mic toward Maria's face, which was ashen and showed streaks of makeup that had been carried astray by tears.

"We were driving out to Jersey," Maria said. "We'd picked up our kids, then gotten through the tunnel and were turning onto, oh I don't know. A car pulled up behind us, and one stopped in front of us. It was planned. They ignored me, ignored my children. They took my husband and... I don't know."

The reporter's face showed deep concern, though it looked fake to Austin. "Did you get a look at their faces, at their vehicles?"

Maria said, "A white and a black SUV. They wore masks. It all happened fast."

The shot cut back to the news anchor, who assured viewers they'd be staying on top of the story and would bring them more details as soon as they had them.

Sven sighed and muted the TV. "Crime. It's bad out there."

Austin took a slow, steady breath. "Yeah," was all he said, his mind racing, his chest tightening. Jorge had known he was in danger, but that hadn't been enough. The fact that Maria and the children had been left alone confirmed what Austin suspected. These weren't blood-crazed murderers, otherwise they would have killed Jorge along with his whole family on sight. This was a professional operation, out to silence anyone who might know about it. And Austin had no doubt that Jorge would be tortured until he gave them everything he knew.

After a moment, he excused himself to head up to bed. Sven didn't look away from the muted TV as Austin left, but Mary was in the hallway blocking his path up the stairs.

"There's something I want to say to you." Her face wore a slight frown. She gestured toward the bench in the foyer.

Austin sat where she directed, facing the door where he'd come in. His coat was still on the hook where he'd hung it and part of him wanted to grab it and run the hell out of there. Head back to New York, to New Jersey and... and *what*? Look for Jorge? He had no leads, no ideas. Nothing. Surely Maria gave any relevant descriptions to the police and they were doing all they could.

Mary seemed determined to tell him something. "Austin. Tommy, look at me."

She stood over him and he looked up.

"Losing a child is the deepest pain anyone can feel," she said. "I know that agony well. Too well. But I also know Fiona, and how deeply she loved you. Sometimes I think I saw it more than you did. I promise you this: She's cheering you on to embrace life and find joy again."

Austin looked away, his eyes drifting toward a patch of bright red fabric sticking out from under a sea of coats on the rack. He focused on it intensely to keep the tears from coming.

"It would honor her memory for you to do so," Mary continued. "To actually *live*. I need to see her light shine on through you, to know her spirit carries forward. She would want you to feel happiness. And Sven and I want you to know happiness, too." She took his shoulders, her tone turning forceful, though not quite angry. "It's your *responsibility* now to grasp hold of life, not just for yourself, but for her, and the rest of us. That's how we keep her memory alive."

She didn't wait for his reply. She patted him on the back and shuffled toward the TV room, from which Austin could still hear the low voices from the newscast.

"Wait," Austin said.

She turned.

"On the wall there, under all the other coats and scarves, is that Fiona's red peacoat?"

Mary turned, nodded, then turned back to Austin. "We've left it there the whole time. Maybe it's time you take it."

Mary moved a few coats that were covering it on the rack, then handed the jacket to Austin.

His throat tightened. His chest ached.

It was a deep red peacoat of fine wool, one Fiona had worn for at least a few years.

And it smelled like her.

～

Austin sat on the edge of the bed, Fiona's jacket spread across his lap. Her mother's words ran through his head, especially one phrase.

Sometimes I think I saw it more than you did.

Something about that hit him hard, harder than he thought anything could. If someone had asked him, *did Fiona love you?* he would have said, "Sure. Of course she did."

He knew that.

But did he?

Sitting there in the dark room it occurred to him that he didn't know that, had *never* known that. He'd been willing to believe that she'd been having an affair with Jorge based on a few incriminating letters and travel arrangements. For that, he'd discounted years of marriage, of something close to happiness.

He knew then that he'd felt all along as though he didn't deserve her. She was like a polished diamond and he was a pebble on the beach. Nothing wrong with a pebble, but it was no diamond.

He pulled the coat in and smelled it and, just like that, Fiona was back.

It was not unlike the times Austin went to sit in the back of the little community church in Hansville. He went there because something in the smell of the place triggered his synesthesia, made him feel that Fiona was present. Usually his synesthesia came with tastes and feelings. When he was in that church, though, Fiona returned because of something in the smell—maybe the age of the wooden floor, mixed with the paint, mixed with... he didn't know.

He'd never been able to explain it, but this time it was easy.

It was the smell of her that still clung to this jacket. The only things of hers that he'd kept—her typewriter, the plaque she'd left on her desk that now hung from the wall of his kitchen—none of those had the smell of her.

He pulled the jacket tight around his face and felt the tears starting to come.

Then he felt something hard, like a jagged button in the wrong place, stabbing at his face. Fumbling in the dark, he moved his fingers along the collar, tracing the shape. It wasn't a button. It was long and narrow and uneven like... he wasn't sure.

He leaned over and flipped on the bedside lamp, studying the dark lining on the inside of the jacket. Where the object was, the threads did not match perfectly. The black stitches were a little darker. More recent.

He ran his hands along the object again. Unless he was crazy, he was feeling the shape of a key.

Quickly but gently, he dug into the seam with his fingernail. Then, when he'd loosened enough threads, he tore it open. A small silver key had been sown into the lining of the jacket, held in place by a triple loop of black thread through its keyring hole.

Austin held it in his hand, mouth half open in disbelief.

He vaguely remembered a trip Fiona had taken to see her parents sometime before she died. A week, maybe two weeks before. It hadn't registered as especially significant at the time. Since they were so close by, sometimes Fiona came up from their New York City apartment for brief visits. Often Austin came along, but not every time. Not when he was busy on a case.

Why would she have sewn a key into the lining of her favorite jacket, and why would she then leave it at her parents' house? A hundred possibilities raced through his mind, but nothing that seemed plausible.

He lay on the bed, exhaustion hitting him all at once. Gripping the key tightly, he felt himself nodding off as visions of Maria's tear-streaked face ran through his mind alongside visions of the video of Javier. Mingled with these real memories were imagined scenes of Fiona walking through the door and hanging her coat on the hook, of her sewing the key into the lining, of Jorge tied up in a trunk somewhere or in the back of a warehouse, absorbing kicks and punches as his captors demanded to know where Thomas Austin was, along with anyone else who'd been looking into the case.

He was far from perfect, but one thing he took pride in was that he never quit. He had a grim determination, almost a mantra, that in everything he tried he would accept any amount of failure, any number of setbacks. He might not always succeed, but he wouldn't stop. He would *never* stop.

As sleep overcame him, his memories and visions grew more dreamlike and he saw himself getting off an airplane in Seattle, Kendall meeting him at the airport, and Run sprinting into his arms and barking in a way that somehow communicated that it was okay that he'd quit this time, and that he'd never have to return to the east coast again.

CHAPTER NINE

PINK-GRAY LIGHT CREPT in through the open curtain as Austin turned the key over and over in his hand.

Perched on the edge of the bed, he let his gaze drift out the window towards the churning ocean. For half a second he imagined himself walking out to the shore, standing for a long time, then tossing the key in the ocean and deciding once and for all to take Mary's advice: to put the case behind him and move on with his life.

It was like a scene from a movie. One that Austin wouldn't bother watching.

Instead, he passed the key from hand to hand, studying it.

It was a peculiar shape, flat and small, with a rectangular head and a mere three notches on the blade, not a conventional house key.

He unlocked his phone and tapped "types of keys" into the search bar. Despite the many images populating his screen—house keys, cash register keys, car keys, old-style ornamental room keys—none matched the unique key he held.

He thought about why Fiona might have a secret key. What

was she hiding? He searched lockbox keys, gym locker keys, safe keys, and, finally, P.O. box keys.

As he scrolled through the results of this last search, a particular image caught his attention. A flat key, simplistic in its design, with a rectangular bow and few cuts. The similarity to Fiona's key was uncanny.

He tapped on the image, leading him to a site detailing information about U.S. postal box keys. The site revealed that these keys were standardized, cut by specialized machines, and each uniquely corresponding to a single P.O. box number.

Austin knelt by the bedside table, holding the key under the lamp. The worn edges suggested frequent use. But the key was unmarked, save for a few scratches.

One thing he was certain of was that they'd never had a P.O. box and that Fiona had never mentioned it. It was the kind of thing he would have remembered simply because it was so out of character.

So why would Fiona have a P.O. box key sewn into her jacket? And why would she leave the jacket it was sewn into at her parent's house?

The answer came as soon as he asked himself the question.

Because there was something important in it, something that was part of her investigation, and she wanted it far away from their home. Most likely she'd gotten the P.O. box at some local post office under the cover of one of her weekend trips to see her parents.

Any thought of going back home vanished in an instant. He knew what he needed to do next.

Downstairs, Fiona's brother James was having breakfast alone. "Mind if I grab a cup of coffee?" Austin asked, gesturing to the half-full French press on the table.

James looked up from his newspaper. "Sure thing. And take a muffin, too."

"Thanks." Austin sat and helped himself to coffee and a muffin. "Mary and Sven are..."

"Out on their walk," James said. "Three miles every day. Like clockwork."

This was fine by Austin. He didn't want to involve them anymore than he already had and, rude as it might be, he planned to head out immediately, without saying goodbye. "Olive still asleep?"

James folded the paper and set it on the table. "She's hitting that age where it goes from me wishing she'd sleep in so I can get stuff done to me wishing she'd get up so she doesn't sleep her life away."

Austin didn't know what to say, so he said, "Being a parent must be hard. I can barely handle raising a dog."

"They say having kids is like ripping your heart out and watching it walk around outside your body." He shook his head. "What they don't tell you is that you also find out that you're not under any control of your heart. And you never were."

They ate and drank coffee in silence for a while, then Austin asked, "When was the last time you saw Fiona?"

James gave him an odd look. "Why?"

"Just wondering."

James shook his head. "You're still trying to solve it, aren't you?"

Austin shrugged. The truth was, he was trying to see if James knew anything about her last trip to her parents' house or, better yet, the key.

James glanced around the silent house, suddenly nervous as though someone could be eavesdropping. "I promised myself, promised her, I'd never say anything."

Austin went cold, looked up. "Say anything about what?"

A pained look crossed James' face and he ran a hand through his thick blond hair. "The submarine."

Austin stood and refilled his coffee, then sat in the chair right next to James. "Why did you promise, *what* did you promise? James, please tell me what you know."

James pressed two fingers into his plate, sticking moist muffin crumbs to the tips and leaving them there. Austin knew he had various nervous habits and, despite being in his late-thirties, playing with his food was one of them. "The last time I saw Fiona was a couple weeks before she died. I was here with Olive and Fi showed up unannounced, saying she had come for dinner. I still don't really know why she was here but I overheard her having a call. She was pacing out there on the lawn and I was upstairs with my window open. You know how brothers and sisters are. I could *tell* something was wrong from her voice. She mentioned a Navy submarine. The USS Sea Prowler. The next morning I asked her about it casually. She said it was just something for work. I pressed a little bit because we are near the Navy base and so I put two and two together." He flicked the crumbs off his fingers, back onto the plate. "Naturally, I began wondering what the heck her job as assistant district attorney in New York City could have to do with the Navy, but she stonewalled me."

Austin tried to stay calm, but he was feeling a rush of curiosity, and also anger. "Why didn't you tell me this earlier?"

"She made me promise not to tell anyone. Said it was no big deal, but it was confidential, for work. Honestly I'd heard her take work calls before and it didn't seem all that unusual. She was always stressed about something for work. When the police interviewed me after she died, I mentioned it. Nothing ever came of it, I guess."

Olive called for her dad from the other room. Austin couldn't quite make out the words but he thought it might have been, "Dad! Food! Orange juice."

"The queen has risen," James said, smiling at Austin, half embarrassed. Then he called back, "Soup's on in here, sweetie!"

"I don't want *soup* for breakfast!" Olive yelled in a sing-song voice.

James continued, now addressing Austin, "On that same trip, before Fiona left, she promised to take Olive on the rides at Coney Island." His voice didn't carry any sadness. It was a simple statement of fact, as though he'd either processed all his emotions or managed to stuff them down forever.

Austin stood. There was nothing more to say.

The local post office opened in twenty minutes, and he intended to be there when it did.

CHAPTER TEN

"I'M SORRY, sir, but without proper documentation, we simply *can't* help you."

Austin squinted at the postal worker behind the counter. He was in his twenties, with a round, fleshy face that Austin was finding increasingly difficult not to want to smack. "But I have the key, I have..."

"Please step aside, sir, there's a line forming behind you."

It was no use.

He'd already tried three other post offices and each had given him the same answer. Without the number of the box, he'd need a death certificate and other paperwork showing that he was the executor of Fiona's estate. Then he'd have to fill out a form and wait 2-3 weeks to gain access to the box.

Without that, and without knowing which box the key was for, they wouldn't even confirm that Fiona *had* a P.O. box.

He tapped the key on the counter, determined not to take his frustration out on the man. "Thank you."

Outside, he had an idea. Last night, he hadn't known how Samantha could help, but today he did. Assuming Fiona had taken out the P.O. box in her name, and that it was somewhere local, maybe Samantha or her hacker boyfriend had a way to locate it. If he knew the number and branch, he could walk right in and open it.

He'd tossed his partially-used disposable phones, so he walked to the electronics store on the corner and bought another using cash. He dialed Samantha's number from memory and, when the call went straight to voicemail, left her a message explaining the situation and asking for help.

Next, he planned to find out as much as he could about the USS Sea Prowler. He retrieved his laptop from the trunk of the car and sat at a metal table outside a Starbucks, logging into their Wi-fi.

Before he could run a search, an email popped up.

Call me ASAP.

It was from Kendall.

When Austin dialed her number from his disposable phone, she picked up immediately, her voice high and tight. "Austin, why aren't you picking up your phone?"

"I had to get rid of it and—"

"Nevermind. Run is sick. I'm driving to the vet right now and—"

Austin stood, then immediately felt lightheaded and sat like he'd been kicked in the stomach. "What happened?"

"Everything was fine this morning, we had our walk as usual, she ate, she played with Ralph, but a few hours later, she was crouched down in the kitchen, whimpering. Her abdomen was hard, swollen like severe bloating or something. She flinched when I tried to touch her. She was clearly in pain."

Austin swallowed hard. "Are you driving right now?" He'd heard the low whooshing background noise that usually accompanied calls over car speakers.

"I'm heading to the emergency vet. She vomited twice during

the drive. I'm really worried. Her breathing is fast, shallow. Her eyes... they're glazed, Austin. I called the vet a few minutes ago to tell them I'm coming and they think it might be acute pancreatitis. Or maybe she just ate something she shouldn't and—"

"*Did* she eat something she shouldn't? You know corgis will eat damn near anything if you're not careful."

"I don't... I don't know. I don't think so."

"I'm sorry," Austin said. "I didn't mean to..." He let out a long breath. "I'm just worried."

He remembered when Run was a puppy and would eat sticks, sand, garbage, anything she could reach. Whatever that trait that some dogs have that makes them not eat things that are dangerous to them, Run didn't have it. Over time, she'd gotten much better about it, but he still kept an eye on her and made sure not to leave anything around that could hurt her. "How far away are you, and did they say anything else?"

"They said it's urgent, life-threatening if we don't act fast. I'm five minutes away and—"

Austin heard a horn honking, then Kendall mumbled a few curses.

"Sorry," she said. "I'm almost there. I gotta go. I'll keep you posted, Austin. I promise to call you at this number as soon as there's any news. Answer the phone from now on, would you?"

The line went dead.

Austin couldn't remember the last time he'd had a beer before noon.

He sipped it slowly, trying to breathe, trying to calm himself. He'd found an understated Italian restaurant near where he'd parked his car and sat outside at a table under an awning. The hostess had warned him that it was too cold to sit outside, but he didn't care.

He sipped his beer and slid it back and forth over the check-ered red and white tablecloth, then closed his eyes tight, remembering the day he'd brought home his little corgi pup, before she'd even had a name.

She'd been eight weeks old and the runt of the litter, but something in her personality told him she was the one he was meant to take home. The moment he'd set her down on his kitchen floor, before he'd even had a chance to close the door, she tore off like a bullet out of a gun, ripping through his apartment like she was training for the annual corgi races at the half-time show of a Seahawks game.

The energetic ball of fluff had blitzed laps around his worn futon as the rain pattered against the foggy windows looking out at the beach. Austin scrambled to corral her, but she zipped figure-eights. She was a blur ducking under tables and chairs.

After five minutes of this frenzied chase, Austin collapsed onto the floor, exhausted. The pup rocketed over him, circling back to happily lick his stubbled face. Austin chuckled, catching his breath as she pressed her paws into his chest and face.

Then it hit him.

"Run," he said. "That's what I'll call you. Run!"

She was perpetual motion. Unceasing energy and optimism.

So *Run* it was. And she lived up to it every day, keeping Austin light on his feet with her puppy moxie and Usain Bolt speed. No matter how bad things got, every time she tore off down the beach, tags jingling, Austin shook his head and grinned.

He wasn't grinning now. Wasn't frowning either.

First Javier, then Jorge's disappearance.

Then the key. Then the submarine.

Now Run. She'd always provided a series of tasks he could handle: feed, walk, love, repeat. And more than that, she'd been a friend he could count on. And now he was 3,000 miles away, completely helpless.

One of the things that bothered Austin more than anything else was self-pity. Even when things were at their worst, he knew that he—and most of the people he knew—had it better than most of the people who'd ever lived. He'd studied history and had developed an understanding of just how bad things had been for most people during most of humanity's brief time on earth.

And yet, right now he couldn't help it. He found himself sipping his beer, gripped by self-pity. He found himself asking why. Why all this was happening right now, to him.

Then he found himself thinking about what James said about being a parent. Taking care of Run was the closest thing to raising a child he'd experienced. And now he knew what James meant about having a heart outside your body and not being able to be in control of it.

He swigged his beer again and fell deeper into self-pity.

Fiona had been his heart walking outside of his body and when death took her, he was left with a hole. Run, along with the beaches of Hansville, had done their best to fill it. But the little café had been the only thing truly within his control since he'd lost his wife.

It hadn't been enough.

The thought of harm coming to Run was unbearable. But the void that Fiona's death left couldn't be filled by a thousand corgis.

Austin finished his beer, paid, and walked back toward the car.

He tried texting Kendall multiple times, but she wasn't responding. He couldn't do anything to help Run from where he was now.

All he could do, all he could think to do, was to keep going.

No, he couldn't help Run, but maybe he could do something to find out who killed Fiona. To do that, he had to find out why she was interested in the Navy sub, the USS Sea Prowler.

And he had an idea of where to start. He'd barely registered the mention of the huge security conference when it flashed by on the news the night before.

But he knew someone who was almost certain to be there. And he hoped she still thought of him as a friend.

CHAPTER ELEVEN

AS SOON AS Austin entered the lobby of the hotel, he felt like he was being watched. And chances were, he *was*. Security was tight, in the form of both electronic surveillance and armed private security guards alongside the regular hotel security.

Before driving over, he'd done some research on the conference. First, he'd checked the list of speakers and confirmed that the person he needed help from would be there. Then he'd found the signup form, which was much more complicated than your average conference application.

It had taken him an hour to sign up for a day pass online, then another half an hour to pass security at check-in. Though the event was open to anyone, each attendee had to pass a background check because of all the high-level law enforcement people and politicians in attendance.

The Tri-State Security Symposium, or *T3S*, was the largest gathering of its kind in the Northeast. Hosted bi-annually at the prestigious Marina View Grand Hotel in New Haven, Connecticut, T3S was near the Naval Submarine Base in Groton.

The event brought together top law enforcement from Connecticut, New York, New Jersey, and Massachusetts. The specialized agenda offered presentations and workshops on emerging crime prevention technologies, cybersecurity threats, advancements in forensics, and counter-terrorism strategies. It was a hub of knowledge, where the best minds in security and defense shared insights and breakthroughs.

The purpose of T3S was unity. It fostered cooperation between agencies that typically operated independently. The conference was a networking feast for building contacts, alliances, and partnerships, to share intelligence and collaborate. As the motto on the huge banner in the hotel lobby read: "Stronger Together."

The symposium also featured a vast exhibitor hall. Vendors showcased the latest in drones, body armor, encrypted devices, biometric systems, and other cutting-edge law enforcement technologies. A marketplace of innovation, most of which made Austin feel as though he was falling further behind the times each day.

But it was that marketplace Austin entered.

The cavernous exhibit hall had a towering ceiling and was filled with hundreds of vendor tables and booths, displaying the latest law enforcement technologies. Surveillance drones, encrypted communication devices, robotic bomb disposal units, voxel 3D imaging systems, VR simulators for firearms training, and advanced crowd scanning and threat detection software. The place had it all and left Austin with a funny feeling.

Part of him loved seeing all the fancy new devices, but it made him miss being a uniformed officer. Part of him wished he was back on the beach with Run.

Run.

He'd decided to trust that Kendall was doing everything she could—what other choice did he have?—but he still checked his phone every couple of minutes to make sure he hadn't missed a call or text from her.

All around, attendees mingled through the aisles, some

sampling new tactical gear like bulletproof vests and helmets, others examining cutting-edge forensic tools for crime scene investigation and evidence collection. The hall buzzed with deal-making, networking, and demonstrations of innovative new products and, by the time Austin reached the end of it, he was dizzy and eager to find his friend.

"Well, if it isn't my square-jawed, laughless, boring as-hell-nemesis."

Austin turned to see a woman who looked to be around thirty with short hair, shaved on the sides and purple on top. She'd clearly been addressing him, but he didn't recognize her. She was definitely *not* the one he'd come to see.

She stood. "Thomas Austin? Right?"

He nodded.

"You don't recognize me?"

"I'm sorry, I—"

She folded her arms. "*You're* the reason I went to jail."

He cocked his head. "I'm the reason a lot of people went to jail."

"I thought you'd bailed and headed west once your wife got killed."

Austin was already on the edge, and her comment thrust him over it. With two quick strides he was at her table, leaning over a display of tasers and partially spitting his words. "I don't know who the hell you are, lady, but don't mention my wife to me again. Got it?"

She leaned away and held up a black-handled taser, pointing it at him, but offering up a sly smile to make sure he knew she wasn't going to fire it. "Mara Graves, and don't worry, the safety is on." She said it with a wink.

Austin's eyes widened. He remembered her from maybe ten years earlier. When Austin had caught her brokering illegal deals for missile technology between U.S. manufacturers and Middle

Eastern nations, he'd referred her case to the FBI. Eventually, Federal prosecutors from the Southern District had gotten her.

He hadn't followed the case closely, but, apparently, she was out of prison and working for a specialty taser company.

As though reading his mind, she said, "I got a reduced sentence by turning over info on some other suppliers. Now I'm on the straight and narrow path." She looked over his shoulder, then said. "My boss is over there. Here." She handed him the taser. "Don't worry, the safety's on. But lemme give the spiel so I don't get fired. Pretend you're interested."

Her voice changed slightly into a practiced, sing-songy sales-pitch. "This is our new Hornet stun gun model, the most powerful compact consumer taser on the market. Using our patented ultra-dense lithium-ion MicroBattery technology, the Hornet generates up to twenty percent more voltage than stan-dard stun guns, delivering a stronger incapacitating shock. And its newly designed focusing electrode prongs offer greater accu-racy. The ergonomic shape maximizes portability for concealed carry, while the safety switch and low battery indicator LEDs make operation secure and user-friendly. If you want the power to stop an assailant in their tracks, the Hornet is the stun gun for you." She let out a breath. "Thanks. He's gone. So, what brings you back to the northeast?"

Running into her here made Austin regret having come. It had occurred to him he might run into someone from his past, but he'd convinced himself that a quick in and out would make that unlikely.

"I gotta get to a talk," he said. "Try to stay out of trouble."

She handed him a business card. "Nice seeing you, too. Call me sometime. I can get you twenty percent off one of these babies."

∽

Austin found room 104 in the corner and stood in the back. It was nearly 2 pm and the talk should be ending soon.

The room was only half full, and the speaker seemed to be wrapping up. Apparently the lecture topic wasn't the most popular: *Best Practices for Evidence Collection and Cyber Forensics in Maritime Environments.*

She was as he remembered her: tall, with long, straight black hair and a direct, no frills manner of speaking accompanied by an occasional bite of dry humor. "I've gone over how maritime environments present unique challenges for cyber forensics—connectivity issues, jurisdictional issues, systems diversification —so I'd like to conclude with some thoughts about cyber forensics in general. This field is all about following the digital breadcrumbs that criminals leave behind. As hackers and online scammers grow more sophisticated, law enforcement needs the tools and know-how to track them down. Forensic analysts comb through mountains of data to identify those clues. Like putting together a jigsaw puzzle, we piece together deleted files, encrypted messages, and network activity logs. Sounds fun, right?"

There were a few courtesy laughs from the audience, and the speaker smiled before continuing. "Anything that can help us reconstruct what happened in the commission of a particular crime. Of course, that data isn't much use in court unless we back it up with impeccable evidence collection and handling, cryptographic verification, and testimony. But with cybercrime on the rise, these forensics skills are now mission-critical, whether at sea or on land. We have to illuminate the shadowy corners of the web where all sorts of illegal activity is happening. Think of this job as the CSI of the internet. Except, you know, with a lot more Reddit memes and Twitter snark."

The audience laughed for real at that one, and Austin even chuckled.

She was a good speaker and, under normal circumstances, he

would have regretted missing most of her talk. But he wasn't there for the information. He was there because she had a connection to the Navy that might offer him some information about the USS Sea Prowler.

When she finished, Austin waited in the back as a few stragglers asked followup questions or exchanged business cards with her. When the last attendee walked away, she headed for the door, but paused when she saw him standing there, leaning against the wall.

Austin didn't wait for her to approach. He walked right up to her. "Symone Aoki, I thought I might find you here."

"Oh my... what? Austin? What are you doing here?" She leaned in and gave him a hug. "Are you back in law enforcement? Back on the east coast?"

"No, actually I came here looking for you."

"I haven't seen you since... well..."

He knew.

They both knew.

CHAPTER TWELVE

THE GARDEN COURTYARD was an oasis tucked away in the center of the hotel's convention facilities. Stone pathways wound through manicured shrubs and trees, many showing the burnt orange and red hues of autumn. Maples and oaks spread half bare branches towards the open sky, the afternoon sunlight filtering through in shards.

As Austin led the way along a walkway, the voices from the convention faded into the background, replaced by the gentle trickle of fountains and the whisper of the breeze through leaves. Sculpted hedges created small private alcoves throughout the courtyard. In one, a stone bench sat encircled by bushes with a few stubborn flowers still blooming despite the cold.

"I'm not going to pretend like I'm not here for a favor," he began. "And I'm not going to pretend that I'm not desperate."

"Okay," Sy said. "But..."

"It'll be easier if you just let me embarrass myself before you shoot me down."

She angled her head toward him slightly, a quizzical look on her face, but said nothing.

"That came out wrong," he said. "I'm not interested in dating you, I—"

Noticing the look on her face, he stopped himself. "Sorry, that came out wrong, too. I mean I'm not here *right now* trying to date you. I need help with a case."

"Shocking that you didn't go into public speaking as a profession," Sy said, laughing. "But seriously, chill out."

The smell of damp earth and dried leaves hung in the cool air. As they strolled along a curve in the path sheltered by the boughs of a willow, its trailing branches brushed their shoulders. They followed the path around a bubbling fountain, a stone whale at its center sending water flowing down the figure of what appeared to be a Greek God. "That Poseidon?" Austin asked.

Sy shrugged. "That what you came here to ask me?"

Austin stopped and sat on a wooden bench. Sy sat as well.

He met her eyes, hoping the intensity of the brief time they'd spent together might make her give him the benefit of the doubt. "The USS Sea Prowler."

He watched her eyes, which betrayed nothing.

"I have reason to believe that there is some connection between that particular sub and a huge case, a—"

"I saw the story in the *Times*, about your wife. Fiona, right?"

Austin nodded.

"I saw that. Is that why you're here?"

He nodded again.

Sy looked up, thinking. "You came across something that makes you think the Sea Prowler is connected to her murder?"

"To a joint operation between the FBI, the NYPD, and her office, the Manhattan district attorney's office. To the case that got her killed. That story was just the beginning of a new phase. At least one person connected to the case has died in the last few days. Another, a friend of mine, is missing. I don't know how many others are dead, but I doubt that number is zero."

She stood, then folded her arms. "Wait, you came to the conference just to see if I'd help you because of my Navy connections?"

He tried to sound light. "Well, last time we worked together it went super well, remember?"

She frowned. "Last time I ended up in the hospital." She blushed and Austin figured she was thinking about what he was thinking about.

After a multi-day investigation that had nearly landed them both in the grave, they'd *kissed* in the hospital. A kiss that had been interrupted by a gunshot.

After the case came to a resolution, he'd assumed they might go out on a real date. Instead, she'd told him that she'd been transferred back to Massachusetts. Though they'd texted a few times since, neither of them had the time or energy for a long distance relationship and Austin now assumed they'd both been caught up in the moment.

"I'm gonna save you some time," Sy said. "No."

Austin had told himself that he'd only ask once. He hated asking for help, hated begging, and not just because it was embarrassing. He hated putting her in the position of doing something outside the bounds of her job. Something that might compromise her position with the Navy.

"Thanks anyway." Austin stood and shoved his hands in his pockets. "Your talk was good, by the way. You're funnier than I expected. You're the one who should have gone into public speaking as a profession."

She scrunched her nose up a little. "You weren't supposed to give up that easy."

"I... what?"

"In my mind, which is a little over-active right now, because of the two Diet Cokes I guzzled to get amped up before my talk, I imagined you giving me some prepared speech about how if it was my husband's death I was investigating, you would help me."

She looked embarrassed, and Austin realized he was giving her some kind of look. "Anyway, that's where my mind went and then I imagined myself agreeing to help you because, it's true, if it were my husband—and if his death was anything other than a tragic accident—I don't think I would be able to stop looking into it either." She walked over to the willow tree and tugged gently on one of the branches, then turned back to face him. "But I wanted you to have to talk me into it."

"I still could. If that would help."

"Nah, let's just skip all that." She glanced down at her watch, a thin silver band with numerals he couldn't make out. "I have a few things to do. Meet me out front at six."

PART 2

A SPECIAL KIND OF ANGUISH

CHAPTER THIRTEEN

SET along the Thames River in southeastern Connecticut, the sprawling Naval Submarine Base New London covered over 680 acres and employed over nine thousand people.

Established in 1868 and home to fifteen nuclear-powered submarines as well as the Navy's Nuclear Power Training Unit, New London was the primary East Coast submarine hub for the US Navy. Its location off Interstates 95 and 395 enabled swift submarine deployments up and down the Atlantic coast and beyond.

As a kid, Austin had lived here with his parents for a year. He thought of it as more of a small city because it included facilities like an administrative support complex, a chapel, a commissary, and a hospital. But approaching it after sunset, one wouldn't have known any of that.

As Austin pulled up to the nondescript gate, the place looked quiet, even peaceful.

Sy leaned across the center console and handed her ID to the uniformed guard in the security building, then spent a few minutes filling out a visitor form.

After handing it to Austin, who handed it to the guard, she

said. "Commander James Kellermen should have called down about this, I believe."

The guard nodded.

Austin handed him his ID, then rolled up the window. "I appreciate this."

"The XO owed me a favor. Long as you stay with me and don't leave the records building, we're good. Should just take a few minutes. Since you're former law enforcement with a clean record... wait, you *do* have a clean record, don't you?"

Austin grinned. "Well, there was the car I stole back in the late nineties. Did two years for that. Then I got involved with the wrong crowd and was busted running moonshine up in the hills outside Arkansas. Plus a few other things. So besides the five or six felonies I committed as a young man, I'm good."

She chuckled. "Yeah, I meant *besides* those. Anyway, I had to tell a little white lie to Commander Kellermen, that I'm bringing you in for an interview on a pending case. Shouldn't be an issue though."

The guard leaned out of the booth and tapped the window, then handed Austin a pass and waved them through.

Sy directed him into the parking lot and he parked in front of a building marked with a small sign that read: *Archives*.

Sy said, "We'll start with the records in physical form since digitization is still in process. It's weird, but sometimes it's easier to find stuff on paper."

This didn't make much sense to Austin, but it was her territory and she knew what she was doing.

The building's exterior was made of red brick and lined with streaks of gray concrete, its military precision present in the orderly rows of windows. The American flag, lit from below and fluttering against the dark sky atop a flagpole, added a touch of color to the otherwise austere surroundings.

Sy paused at the bottom of the steps. "We need to get more specific. On a sub of that size, we're talking hundreds of thou-

sands of pages of records. Ship's logs. Personnel files. Mainte-
nance records. Deployment records. Communication records.
Incident reports."

"Let's start with incident reports," Austin said, "as that's
most likely how she heard about it. 2015 to 2020, I'd guess, the
years before Fiona was looking into it. But it could be further
back. And is there any way to sort them by severity? Two sailors
fighting over a girlfriend or a game of cards isn't the kind of
thing she would have been interested in."

Sy frowned. "Not that I know of. This could get tricky."

Inside the archives building, Sy strode up to a small booth
that guarded the entrance to a long hallway. "Hey, Graber, how'd
the softball game go?"

The man behind the window didn't stand or lower his feet
from the desk. "We lost. Seven to three."

She frowned. "Bummer. Pitching the way you do, I thought
for sure you'd annihilate them. I told you not to go out drinking
the night before."

"That's not why we lost."

She tilted her head in mock sympathy. "It's just 'cause you're
bad, then?"

"Shut up," he said, smiling. "We'll get 'em next year. Who's
this?"

Austin reached his hand under the window. "Thomas
Austin," he said.

"He's here to talk to me about an old incident. USS Sea
Prowler. But first we're looking for any connected incidents so
we need records of any major dust-ups during the Sea Prowler's
deployment starting in 2020 and, well, just working backwards
from there. I understand these reports might not be sorted by
severity. Could you guide me to the appropriate section or
provide any tips for identifying the more serious incidents?"

Graber stood and glanced at Austin. "Follow me," he said.

"That's a helluva range without being more specific, but I'll get you started."

They wound through narrow aisles lined with imposing shelves that stretched two stories high, the wood dark and scarred by time. Graber's movements were economical, as though he was trying to expend the minimum amount of energy, or maybe he was just tired from his softball game.

Leading them to a heavy wooden table situated under the glow of a pair of lamps, he said, "Have a seat," then headed through a low gate into the archives.

Sy was silent, and Austin tapped his fingers on the table, more nervous than he wanted to be. Polished by decades of use, its surface shone like glass, etched with spirals and markings that hinted at the years of notetaking that had traced patterns into its woodgrain.

A few minutes later, Graber returned, a library cart creaking under the weight of a dozen thick binders. Their labels leapt out, naming the USS Prowler and proclaiming the span of years contained within those pages. He set the first four binders down with a muffled thud. "That's 2017 to 2020. Take your time. I'll get the rest."

With a nod, Sy opened the binder, the crisp whisper of turning pages the only sound in the hushed room. When Graber was gone, Sy slid Austin a binder as well.

Austin began scanning the pages, a bit overwhelmed. But immediately he noticed something in the records. "This sub was all over Southeast Asia. That fits."

Sy nodded, but said nothing.

It was a good start, but Austin realized quickly that a start was *all* it was. There were hundreds of incidents listed in these pages, most of them minor. Breach of protocol, deliberate equipment damage, injuries caused by negligence. All of them were serious when seen in the context of a nuclear sub, but none of them amounted to evidence of a massive conspiracy to bring drugs into the country through southeast Asia.

"You say not all this stuff is digitized yet?" Austin asked. "How is that possible? I'm no computer genius, but even I know we could search for drug-related incidents if we—"

"Shhh," Sy scolded.

"What?"

"It's not only that they haven't all been digitized." She glanced around nervously, then leaned in and whispered. "It's that I don't want to leave any digital record of our search."

That made sense, Austin thought. After all, she *had* just given a talk on digital forensics.

She stood and handed him two more binders. "So let's get reading."

By eleven o'clock they'd gone back to 2014 and Austin had compiled a list of eight names, eight incidents that could possibly have landed on Fiona's radar. Sy had her own list, another five names.

But they'd only made it through half of the binders and had only had time to skim many of the incidents, dismissing anything minor without reading the details.

"I'm gonna... do you know what?" Sy asked. "I think I'll... yeah... I will... it'll be fine."

Austin was confused. "Are you talking to me, or just kinda thinking out loud?"

"It's late, we've got some names. I'm just gonna try a few quick searches." She stood and took Austin's list, then headed for the door.

Confused, he followed her out. Telling Graber she'd be back in a bit, she headed down the hall to where a glass doorway led into a room full of computers. "The digital archives," she said. "You'll have to wait out here."

Austin shoved his hands in his pockets. "Fine by me, but what about—"

"Quiet. Lemme do this before the smart part of my brain returns and tells me it's a bad idea."

She typed in a key code and the door unlocked. Looking back at Austin through the window, she sat at a computer near the door as it clicked shut behind her.

For the next ten minutes, Austin watched her type, shaking her head periodically and crossing names off the list. He leaned against the wall, watching the back of her head.

Then something changed in her demeanor. All of a sudden she cocked her head to the side and brought her hand to the back of her neck, a habit she had when she was thinking hard. Austin had seen her do this twice before. Once when she was considering clues and once when she was deciding which donut to buy during a visit to the Norwegian bakery in downtown Poulsbo.

She glanced back at him, smiling.

She had something. He knew it.

Waaaa Waaaaa Waaaaa

It was the piercing sound of an alarm, coming from the area where they'd checked in with Graber.

Waaaa Waaaaa Waaaaa

Sy started scribbling on her notepad, then glanced back at him again. She mouthed something to him once, twice, then turned back to the screen.

Waaaa Waaaaa Waaaaa

He wasn't sure, but he thought she was saying, "Get the hell out of here."

CHAPTER FOURTEEN

AUSTIN FROZE FOR HALF A SECOND, then tasted hot sauce in his mouth—a bright, spicy flavor that made his forehead bead with sweat and his whole body tingle. It came with a feeling somewhere between resolve and panic.

Either way, it kicked him into gear.

With one more glance at Sy, he took off at a brisk pace down the hall, back in the direction of the room where they'd been examining the binders.

His plan was to duck into the room and...

And what?

He was thinking through his options when he heard heavy footsteps coming toward him down the hall. There was nowhere to go, so he braced himself for... for what?

Two men with jaws as square as their shoulders appeared from around a corner and hurried past him, completely ignoring him as they headed for the computer room.

~

Sy's eyes darted back and forth across the words on the screen. She'd searched seven names and the seventh, Joey Green, had triggered the alarm. Of course, this had told her she'd hit on something important, but it had also frozen her screen.

A second later, she'd heard the alarm.

She knew what was happening, and it wasn't good. It also wasn't the first time. From time to time a particular document got reclassified such that her access was denied. And, even less frequently than that, a search triggered something within the system that meant she'd crossed a line.

This time, though, her access hadn't simply been denied. Her screen had frozen with the front page of Joey Green's personnel file visible.

She yanked out her phone and, pretending to scroll—in case she was being recorded, which she knew she likely was—snapped a couple photos of the screen, then sat calmly and read through the information a second time as she waited for whatever or whoever was coming for her in response to that alarm.

U.S. NAVY - DEPARTMENT OF THE NAVY - OFFICIAL MILITARY PERSONNEL FILE

Full Name: Joey Dimitri Green

Rate/Rank: CS2 (Culinary Specialist Petty Officer 2nd Class)

Service Number: N193-4561

Status: Discharged

Dates of Service: 2010 - 2017

Primary MOS (Military Occupational Specialty): Culinary Specialist (CS)

Basic Personal Details:

Date of Birth: 1991-07-27

Place of Birth: Trenton, New Jersey

Home of Record: Trenton, New Jersey

Entry Place: MEPS New Haven, CT

Recruit Training: Recruit Training Command, Great Lakes, Illinois (2010)

A School: Culinary Specialist "A" School, Fort Lee, Virginia (2011)

Duty Stations:

1.USS Los Angeles (SSN-688), Pearl Harbor, Hawaii (2011-2013)

2.USS Sea Prowler, Naval Submarine Base New London, Connecticut (2013-2017)

Deployments:

1.Western Pacific Deployment (2011-2012, USS Los Angeles)

2.Southeast Asia Deployment (2012-2013, USS Los Angeles)

3.Arctic Deployment (2014-2015, USS Sea Prowler)

4.Southeast Asia Deployment (2015-2017 USS Los Angeles)

Awards and Decorations:

1.Navy and Marine Corps Achievement Medal (2014)

2.Good Conduct Medal (3 awards, 2012, 2014, 2016)

Separation Information:

Date of Discharge: 2017-05-15

Place of Discharge: Naval Submarine Base New London, Connecticut

Discharge Status: Dishonorable

Reason for Discharge: REDACTED

Additional Information:

Education: Associates Degree in Culinary Arts, Coastline Community College, 2011

Civilian Certifications: ServSafe Certification, 2011

Even though she knew she was about to be escorted out, and feared what would happen after that, she couldn't help but connect Joey Green's story with what Austin had told her about the case. As she pieced it together in her mind, she became fairly certain this was the guy Fiona had been in the area to find out about.

By the time she heard the door creak open behind her, she was convinced they had stumbled upon a crucial piece of the drug trade that carried narcotics from Southeast Asia to the East Coast via nuclear submarine.

"Symone Aoki." The voice at the door sounded firm, but not especially threatening. "Please stand and turn around."

CHAPTER FIFTEEN

SAMANTHA WATCHED Ridley's face drop as Andrea hit send on the email. The opposition research she'd spent hours digging up was on the way to every news outlet in the state.

"No going back now that we're *in* it," he said, so softly it was almost to himself.

Andrea looked at her boss, optimism and reassurance all over her face. "We didn't have a choice, Rid. They started this fight. We couldn't just stand here with our hands in our pockets." She stood and began making grand gestures. It was as though she was trying to convince herself that they'd done the right thing. "My dad told me, 'Never start a fight. But if someone *else* starts a fight, be damn sure you finish it.' With Samantha's help, I think we may be able to."

Ridley looked up. "What happened to *Light Dims Darkness?*"

Everyone was quiet.

Samantha bit her lip. She knew that had been one of the slogans Ridley's campaign had used, a nod to his belief in ignoring all the mudslinging and dirty tricks of a typical political campaign in favor of taking the high road.

Finally, Andrea ran a hand over her crisp white button-down.

"It will, Ridley. I promise your personal light will dim some of the darkness. But only if we win." She nodded up at the countdown clock she'd affixed to the wall. It read 56 hours and 12 minutes. Since Washington was a vote-by-mail state, some voting was already underway. They had 56 hours until it ended.

Next to it, the latest numbers from their internal polling, which was at least a couple days more current than the polls conducted by news organizations.

Grayson Daniels: 33%
Ridley Calvin: 29%
Jeremy Carter: 28%
Undecided: 9%

Ridley's number had dropped a couple points since the release of the opposition research into his past, despite a series of appearances defending his record and explaining the situations.

Samantha had been able to dig up more dirt on Ridley's two opponents than even *she'd* thought possible. And she had no doubt that—unless the press ignored it—it would get Ridley those points back, and maybe enough to win him the election.

Sheriff Daniels, it turned out, had received DUIs in no less than three different states. One of them had occurred in Oregon only a week earlier and—somehow—remained out of the news. DUIs in three states probably wasn't a world record, but she thought it might be for a gubernatorial candidate. Even though Daniels had admitted to occasional problems with alcohol, he'd claimed both that he'd only had the one DUI, and that he'd received treatment and was now sober. Both were stone cold lies. And nobody wanted a drunk behind the wheel of a car *or* running the state.

Daniels also received at least three million dollars in donations from shady organizations out of state, operating at the very edge of campaign finance laws. She was still tracking down the details of the organizations that were funding him, but it didn't look good. She and Andrea hoped that, by sharing what they knew with news outlets, reporters would do their own digging and find more details of his corruption. Once they set things in motion, everything would snowball.

And Carter had quite a few skeletons of his own. Tax evasion, a case that was dropped when he appointed a former IRS agent to his team. And, worse, an assault charge in college that was much more serious than anything Ridley had been accused of. He'd been arrested for assaulting his pregnant girlfriend while drunk, though later she'd changed her story and dropped the charges.

So, despite Ridley's disappointment at having to take the low road, Samantha felt that releasing the information was not only justified, it was necessary. At least as far as she was concerned, Ridley's opponents were far worse than him, and letting people know about it was actually a good thing.

"Keep digging," Andrea said, ushering the others out of the room. At the doorway, she paused. "And Samantha. Really good job. The information you've provided might be the difference in this thing. There's a reason I'm such a hardass about this stuff: it's not small or abstract. It actually *matters*. I know it can seem from afar that all these guys are the same and that no one can make anything better. No one knows what the next years will bring, and having Rid in charge won't suddenly fix everything, but wouldn't you rather have him in the room when the big decisions have to get made?"

Samantha nodded. "And I'm here now, until the end. Whatever you and Rid need."

Andrea smiled and left her alone.

Lucy and Jimmy had returned from their brief honeymoon and Lucy had given her the week off to focus on the campaign. Samantha still didn't care much about politics, but she knew she didn't want either of Ridley's opponents steering state policy.

That meant she was going to do anything she could to get him elected.

As she kicked her bare feet up on the table, her phone rang and she smiled when she saw the caller-ID: *Yotta-Bae*. It was her boyfriend, Chris. "Hey, YB. I did good."

"I knew you would." Chris had gotten his nickname after a pretend lover's quarrel that started with Chris telling her he loved her more than cheese. After that, she'd told him she loved him a gigabyte, and when he'd replied that he loved her a yottabyte, it cemented her nickname for him. She'd called him her Yotta-Bae ever since.

"Turns out," she said, "Carter and Daniels are even more scummy than we knew."

"A scummy politician? I'm thoroughly shocked! I have good news, too. Remember when you said I was a genius?"

She smiled. "Hmm, I have no recollection of that."

"Well, you said it, and it turns out you were right."

"That key?" she asked.

"Check your app."

"You found it?"

"You know how sometimes you tell me I like to do things the hard way?"

Samantha smiled. "Like the time you decided to decrypt that file manually instead of just using the decryption key?"

"But I—"

"Oh, or the time you wrote your own device drivers and firmware code for our smart refrigerator instead of using the manufacturer's software. I mean, did it really need to be 'optimized'?"

"You done?"

She cleared her throat as she opened the Signal app on her laptop. "Yes, so what was it this time?"

"Well, I was stressing about how to ID that woman's P.O. box without hacking the Post Office and potentially getting a one-way ticket to federal prison."

"A wise move," she said. She'd made him promise to try to find a record of Fiona's P.O. box, but made him promise not to do anything illegal.

"I'll spare you all the things I tried that didn't work. Long story short, I ended up trying the dark web. Turns out, some loser hacked the post office a year ago and uploaded the entire P.O. box directory! All I had to do was download that bad boy and ctrl-F 'Fiona Austin.' Bam! You see it?"

She did. He'd sent her the box number and post office address.

"My hands are as clean as a whistle," he said. "Whoever hacked the post office broke the law, but by simply searching available information, I did not. Squeaky clean."

"Hold on," she said. Samantha copied the information, then sent it to Austin's Signal account, which she'd set up for him.

"Spotless." He was whispering now. "Unsullied," he continued.

She breathed a sigh of relief. "Okay. Enough synonyms. Democracy is saved, rockstar private investigator helped. Not a bad day's work. What do you want for dinner? Pizza or Thai?"

"Yes."

"You got it bae, both it is."

CHAPTER SIXTEEN

AUSTIN STOOD with his hands on the table where he and Sy had been reading the binders. He was pretending to read one of the archives, and waiting. He had no idea what was going on, but the men in heavy boots who'd marched past him in the hallway were definitely not heading toward Sy to offer her a medal for a job well done.

Glancing up, he saw the two men again, this time with Sy held in front of them.

He thought about interjecting, but what good would that do? He was on a day pass, Sy was a seasoned NCIS agent, and who knew what the hell rank the guys leading her were.

They didn't seem to care about his presence, and, though he wasn't sure, he thought Sy had given him a careful side-eye, a look of... he didn't know what? Of *emphasis*, maybe. A look that told him to listen to what she'd mouthed at him before. To get out of there. That she didn't need his help.

She'd told him to get out of there, and that's what he'd try to do.

Returning the way he'd come in, Austin stopped at the desk. "Graber, any idea what happened?" He tried to sound casual.

"No idea." Graber shook his head. "If I were you, I'd head out."

"The archives are all on the table. Okay to leave them there?"

Graber nodded. "That siren goes off for one of three reasons. Unauthorized personnel in the building, which isn't the case this time. Glitches, which happen *often* with our damn system. And accessing files beyond your level. My guess is, that's what happened. Assuming it was unintentional, Sy probably gets a slap on the wrist. Everyone respects her, but they have to go through the protocol."

Austin thanked him and walked out into the night, breathing in the fresh, cold air as the wind carried the scent off the water.

Back at his car, he gripped the steering wheel and thought through what Graber had said. He thought of himself as someone who would never leave a colleague behind, never leave a partner behind. So what the hell was he doing? Was he really going to leave her?

This was an unusual situation, though, one he'd never come up against. If Graber was right, she'd be let out soon and she'd contact him. But if he was wrong...

The worst case scenario was that someone high-up in the Navy was involved in this cover-up, someone with real connections to the Namgungs, to the corrupt elements of the NYPD or FBI.

Austin heard his knuckles pop on the steering wheel. He was squeezing it like a stress ball.

He shook his head. There was no way that was the case. He had to believe that this would resolve itself without him, and that Sy knew what she was doing.

He started the car and drove back to the security gate. "Heading out," he said as he rolled down the window.

The man shook his head. "Pull off to the right, sir. You're going to need to come inside."

Austin's throat tightened. But part of him felt relief. Leaving Sy behind hadn't felt right.

Inside the security office, a man in a khaki shirt and black trousers led Austin toward a hard plastic chair. He jotted a few things on a form pinched to a clipboard, then looked up. "I need a report. I'm waiting on a call to let me know if you're free to leave the base, but, in the meantime, can you tell me what happened?"

Austin let out a breath. "I don't really know what happened."

He sighed. "Tell me what you were looking for?"

Austin's mind raced, but quickly landed on what he understood to be the only option: tell the truth.

Even if he hadn't respected the Navy—which he did—he was smart enough to know that lying would do him no good. The rooms they'd been in were surveilled, and clearly something in Sy's search had triggered something that would have been recorded.

So over the next twenty minutes, he told the truth. Most of it, anyway. He left out the details of the Namgung crime family and its possible connection to Fiona's murder, but shared that he was a private investigator looking into a murder and had received a tip that the case may have involved an incident on the USS Sea Prowler.

He made sure to describe it all in a way that would make it appear as though Sy was not breaking any rules, though he figured it was too late to help her if she had.

The guard dutifully took notes, looking up every now and then and nodding. It was clear that he felt little personal stake in the situation.

When the phone in the security office rang, he picked it up immediately. "Okay, yes sir. Yes, sir. Absolutely, sir." He hung up and looked at Austin. "I'll need your pass."

"I assume you can't tell me what's going on?" Austin asked, handing the man his pass.

He frowned. "Sy's a friend, and I'll let her know you left. I've been told to let you leave. You didn't do anything wrong."

"Sy? What's gonna happen to her?"

"I don't know," he said, then continued in a whisper, "I heard them call in an IO Team and a Legal Officer. Doesn't seem good."

CHAPTER SEVENTEEN

AUSTIN STILL HADN'T HEARD from Sy when he reached the post office the following morning.

After leaving the base, he'd driven all the way to New Haven just to switch his car for another one. This time it was a blue minivan, and he'd slept in the back seat at a rest area on Interstate 95.

He hadn't been able to reach Kendall, but had received a message from Samantha on his laptop when he'd finally figured out how to use his disposable cell phone as a Wifi-hotspot. The message was only four lines, but had hit him like a bolt of lightning.

PO Box 781
Cos Cob Post Office
152 East Putnam Avenue
Cos Cob, CT 06807

He didn't have any idea how she'd come across the information, and he didn't want to know. But he was confident it was correct.

He'd arrived ten minutes before they opened, and he smiled

at the woman who unlocked the door to let him in at 9 AM on the nose.

He found box 781 easily and the key worked immediately. All of it seemed easy. Too easy after what he'd been through.

He opened the tiny metal door and peered in, panicking for a moment when it appeared that the box was empty.

Then he saw it. Flat against the bottom of the box was a single, thin envelope. He pulled it out and flinched when he looked at it.

It was a standard size white envelope, and it was marked with Fiona's handwriting. She'd addressed it to the P.O. box. The return address was the apartment they'd shared in New York City.

He looked around, half expecting someone to grab him, to usher him away, to do *something*. He expected an alarm to sound like it had at the naval base.

It couldn't be this easy. Then he reminded himself that he was simply accessing his wife's P.O. box. There was nothing illegal or corrupt about it.

Swallowing hard, he walked out of the post office and returned to the minivan. Locking himself in, he carefully opened the envelope. Inside were two pieces of ivory paper. The first contained a letter, the second a list of names, with a brief paragraph after each name.

He recognized the typeface and the feel of the expensive linen paper. Fiona had typed these pages on her typewriter, the one he still had set up in his apartment back home.

First he scanned the names and the brief descriptions after each one:

---

1. **Cardinal James Dellacorte** - Head of the New York Archdiocese and one of the most influential Catholic leaders in the state. Has longstanding ties to police and city

officials. A church accountant told me that large, unex-plained donations have recently been made to the archdio-cese from an offshore account possibly linked to the cartel.

2. Mayor McKinley - As mayor of NYC, McKinley directs the police department and has huge sway over city policies/operations. Rumored to have ambitions for higher office. Senate. Presidency. Received anonymous tip that the mayor's re-election campaign was partially funded by cartel money funneled through a super PAC.

3. Lieutenant Governor Mark Richardson - As LG, Richardson has connections statewide in law enforce-ment and politics. Positioned to run for Governor soon. Read a report that indicated FBI had wiretaps captured between Richardson and a known cartel associate about "transporting product" from "our friends overseas."

4. FBI Director Walter Perkins - Oversees all FBI field offices in NYC and directs many joint operations with NYPD. Approaching retirement. Bank records show Perkins made numerous trips to Southeast Asia that coin-cided with major drug shipments into New York Harbor.

5. Chief Justice Evelyn Lim - First Asian American chief justice of the New York Court of Appeals. Sway over criminal cases. An informant claimed Lim received bribes to give lenient sentences to cartel members arrested for drug trafficking.

Austin let his eyes fall closed, imagining what it must have been like for Fiona to write those notes. An assistant DA for Manhattan with evidence indicating that those five people—five of the most powerful people in New York, if not the entire country—might be part of a huge organized crime syndicate. Even with help from people like Jorge, she must have felt so alone.

What didn't make sense was that, though each name on the list could potentially be tied to the Namgungs, there was no rock solid evidence. And it wasn't clear who was actually involved in the case.

He hoped the second piece of paper would explain it. So he read the letter.

Investigation into the Namgung crime syndicate reveals deeply concerning corruption and collusion. This Southeast Asian organization is smuggling narcotics into New York City on a massive scale.

The complexity of the operation implies involvement by our own law enforcement agencies—potentially including rogue elements in the NYPD and FBI aiding the syndicate's activities.

The leader of the syndicate goes by the alias "The Magician." True identity remains unknown. Intelligence gathered points to one of five potential suspects, all of whom hold influential positions in government, law enforcement, and/or business.

The depth of corruption is vast, spanning not just criminal networks, but trusted institutions. Pursuing the truth poses professional and personal risks that must be weighed carefully.

However, exposing and prosecuting those responsible for enabling this dangerous enterprise is essential for the safety and justice of our city.

Next steps: Verify intelligence, identify informants, create files on the five potential suspects for cross-reference analysis to determine the identity of "The Magician" from among the five listed.

Austin was stunned. He sat for... he didn't know how long.

The entire time he'd been investigating this case, this letter had been sitting in the pre-paid P.O. box just waiting to be discovered.

Fiona had been working on one of the biggest cases in the history of New York, and it seemed to implicate some of the biggest names in New York government and beyond. She'd been weeks, maybe days from cracking the case, and she'd mailed herself an envelope with the details of her investigation.

When his phone rang he recognized Sy's number and picked up immediately.

"Well," she said. "They let me go, but it appears I'm going to have a lot more free time to help you with the case."

"Why's that?" Austin asked.

"I've been suspended."

CHAPTER EIGHTEEN

AUSTIN MET Sy two hours later after another car swap, a trip through an underground parking garage, and three loops around the block. He was now quite certain that he wasn't being tracked, or followed.

Sy was waiting in a booth in the corner of a little coffee shop when he came in. To his surprise, she looked fairly cheerful as she dug into a steaming bowl of soup.

"Their corn chowder is to die for," she said, crumbling a few crackers into the bowl.

The rich scent of corn and bacon and potatoes reminded Austin how hungry he was.

A waiter appeared and he ordered a bowl for himself, plus a black coffee. A while back he'd had a brief flirtation with eating healthier, but that was out the window now. It wasn't that he was eating poorly. Not exactly, anyway. It was that he was barely eating at all. When he'd put on his shirt that morning he'd noticed himself looking thinner, and not in a good way. He was looking gaunt, dehydrated, like a man not eating well and sleeping in his minivan.

When the waiter left, Austin said, "We both have news, so

who goes first?" He'd mentioned he had something important when they'd spoken briefly, but hadn't given any details.

"I'll start," Sy said. "It'll be quick because I don't know much." She took another few bites of the soup, then launched into it. "So yeah, I got suspended. It's a muck up, to be sure. They're investigating me for looking at some classified file I wasn't supposed to access. Apparently my little mission triggered a security alert, and they flagged my activity as an unauthorized breach. My security clearance has been revoked, pending an investigation, and I'm suspended until they finish their inquiry."

She quieted down when the waiter appeared with Austin's soup.

He took a bite, then another, and another. "This stuff is delicious." He could feel his body perking up as it was hit with much-needed nutrition.

"So yeah," Sy continued, "I'm out of a job for the foreseeable future. But at least you're in the clear."

"So which was the name that triggered the siren?"

"Joey Green. He's a New Jersey kid, joined the Navy back in 2010, straight out of high school. Trained as a culinary specialist. Spent the first few years on the USS Los Angeles out in Hawaii, Western Pacific and Southeast Asia. Then he got transferred to our neck of the woods, assigned to the USS Sea Prowler. Did a couple more tours. Guy even got his culinary arts degree while on active duty. Apparently the dude could cook. Discharged in 2017, but the reason? Now, that's the mystery. That part's been redacted from his file."

"If his name triggered the system, how did you see his file?"

"I only saw the top sheet. My hunch is that someone wanted to know who was attempting to access it, and I couldn't get in any deeper to see why he was discharged."

Austin swirled his spoon around the edge of his bowl. "So, let's assume he's involved in this. What do you think really happened?" Austin asked.

"Oh he's involved. Two ways I can see. Either he was involved in a smuggling operation on board the USS Sea Prowler, or someone else was and he found out about it. Either way, someone high up knew, he was discharged, and his file was tampered with. To protect him and anyone higher up that might have been implicated by what had been in the file."

They ate in silence for a moment, then Sy said. "I should walk away at this point. Technically, I didn't do anything wrong, and chances are that's going to be enough to save my job. They'll probably slow play this thing and give me some redacted version of his file in three weeks, apologizing for the mix up."

Austin sipped his coffee. "So, what are you... It sounds like you want to say something else."

Sy looked at him, her dark eyes piercing. "I don't know. I feel like I've done a lot of good with NCIS, but..." she trailed off and Austin could almost hear the series of "buts" she wasn't saying. He didn't know the specifics, but it was as though she had a dozen dreams she'd never pursued and was thinking through all of them. "I don't know, ever since that day... I don't know... maybe this is my time to leave. I told myself that day I'd leave within a year, and yet..."

Austin swallowed hard. He knew she was talking about the day her husband died.

"It was supposed to be routine underwater welding training," she said after a long silence. "He was one of the leading divers, doing a hull inspection on a submerged submarine at the Bremerton Naval Base. He'd done dozens of dives just like this one. But that day, something went wrong."

She'd mentioned that he'd died by accident during the few days they'd spent together in Washington State, but never told him the details. And he didn't know why she was telling him now.

"They determined later that a welding torch from a previous dive must have damaged his oxygen line, weakening it imperceptibly," she continued. "By the time the crew realized his line was leaking... well, his oxygen had been cut off for over three minutes, ninety feet underwater. The other divers tried to share their lines, but it was too late. When they pulled his body to the surface and got him to the medics, there was nothing they could do. No breathing, no pulse." Her voice shook, but she continued. "He knew the risks. But during a simple training drill because of a damaged oxygen line..." she trailed off.

"I'm sorry," Austin said. There was nothing much else he could say.

"Sometimes I wonder what else I might be doing with my life." She laughed sadly. "We had this plan... it sounds stupid in retrospect."

"Tell me."

"I was gonna leave, take early retirement. Go work at a winery."

"A what?" This was the last thing he expected to hear.

She gave him a sarcastic look. "The place where they smash grapes, ferment them. Put them in a bottle."

"I know, I just..."

"Surprised, right? It was just a dream I had. To do something *totally* different. Something that celebrates life, being human, instead of spending my time delving into the minds and evidence trails of people who destroy it."

Austin was quiet for a long time. "I can understand that. Sometimes I wonder what else I might have done, although I don't think I could have done much else. I guess I did try running a café, and general store, and bait shop. Technically, I guess I still am, though for the last year or so I seem to be getting further and further away from it." Austin stirred his soup and took a small bite before continuing. "Someone said something to me the other day. They were talking about Fiona, but I bet it applies to your husband, too. She said, 'She's cheering you on to embrace life and find joy again.' Now, I don't think Fiona is cheering me on, not exactly. I don't think that's how it works. I think that's a story we tell ourselves to feel better when the people we love are gone and we see someone else we love in pain. I don't know, I think that she'd want me to continue. Yeah, she'd want me to do the next thing." He pulled the envelope out of the inner pocket of his jacket.

Sy looked up as he slid it across the table.

"This letter is a Pandora's box," Austin said. "You could run off and stomp grapes this minute and I wouldn't blame you, or you could go back to the Navy and be none the wiser. If you decide to read what's in there, you'll know what you know and things will get dangerous." He considered this. "*More* dangerous, that is. All I'm saying is, decide whether you want to get out now, before you open it."

Sy held the envelope in her hand and turned it over, inspecting it. "Do you think she'd want you to be doing this?"

Austin shrugged, pretending he didn't understand the question.

Sy didn't buy it. "You know what I mean."

"Do I think she'd want me to keep investigating her murder?"

Sy nodded.

Austin tasted the familiar burnt toast bitterness that came with dread, but this time it also had a nauseating moldy taste that he associated with disgust. The dread was about the future, the disgust was with himself, in the present. "I know for sure she *would not*."

Sy let his words hang there.

"Here's what I think she would say," Austin continued. "She'd say that if I'm doing it to make New York City safer, okay fine. That's a worthy cause. If I'm doing it for revenge, she'd probably tell me exactly what someone else told me a while back: give all the evidence to the NYPD, the FBI, and let them handle it."

"But if the FBI and NYPD are implicated..." Sy trailed off.

"Or the Navy." Austin picked up his spoon to take another

bite, then set it down. "Truth is, I have no idea what I'm doing. Of course Fiona wouldn't want me doing this, but here I am."

"Here *we* are," Sy said, tapping the envelope on the table. "And we may as well get into it."

She reached to open the envelope but Austin stopped her, placing his hand on hers. "Are you sure? Once you see the names in that envelope…" He shook his head. "I don't know which one is behind this, or even for sure that any of them are. But once you see them, you won't be able to unsee them."

"I've seen some bad things, Austin. And, I know what a Pandora's box is."

"If one of the names in that envelope is behind this operation, you've never seen anything like this. No one has."

CHAPTER NINETEEN

SY GUIDED the car smoothly down I-95, the outskirts of New York City materializing before them. Austin watched as the green expanses of Connecticut receded, replaced by the urban sprawl of the metropolis.

"How far is the dealership?" she asked.

Austin glanced at the map on her phone. "Says fifty-eight minutes. Take the bridge."

Entering the city via the Throgs Neck Bridge, Austin took in the sight of the East River, its waters reflecting the fading sunlight. As a rookie cop, he'd once seen a man jump to his death into that river. He'd been working a fender bender on the Brooklyn Bridge and had looked up just as a man leapt from his car and jumped off. It stunned Austin, saddened him, and hardened him to what could often be a bleak, depressing job. It was said that only one in a thousand survived a jump from the Brooklyn Bridge. The man he'd seen had died on impact.

He thought about that man every time he saw the East River. Now, the city's skyline loomed above it in the distance, a stark silhouette against the evening sky.

He and Sy had gone over the contents of the envelope at the

table and talked through their options. After some back and forth, they'd settled on a three-part plan. Part one was to get in touch with Mara Graves, the taser dealer Austin had run into at the security conference. If Austin was right, she was not as legitimate as she wanted to appear, and they needed some things she might be able to provide. When he'd called her using the number on the business card she'd shoved into his pocket, she'd chatted him up like an old friend and said to come right down to their company headquarters in the Financial District in Lower Manhattan.

Next, they'd find somewhere to stay in the city, then try to locate Joey Green, the cook from the USS Sea Prowler.

If they were lucky, they could get him to talk about his discharge, about how and why he'd been busted. And if they were *really* lucky, they could get him to talk about the names on Fiona's list, maybe even identify which of those five was The Magician.

After that, well, they hadn't thought that far ahead.

The third piece of their plan was to look into the five names on Fiona's list, though they didn't want to do that until they knew they were doing so securely. That's where Mara came in. Austin also planned to ask Samantha for help.

As they approached the Financial District, the cityscape morphed into a forest of skyscrapers, their sharp angles cutting the sky. Sy turned onto the district's narrower streets, the city's history palpable in the older stone and brick buildings.

A+ Security's corporate headquarters sat in a modern glass and steel building squeezed between two older buildings of elegant gray stone.

"That building looks like an iPhone squeezed between two rocks," Sy said.

Austin smiled. "You really are funnier than I knew." Looking through the building's glass facade, he could see people moving about, though he didn't see Mara.

She'd told him to text when he arrived so, as Sy parked, he sent Mara a message. A moment later, he saw her bright purple hair emerge through the large glass door.

Austin got out of the car and Mara nodded down the block. "Follow me," she said. "I'm thinking this isn't a meeting we want to have where everyone can see."

~

"This feels like a drug deal," Sy said, leaning on a stack of cardboard boxes.

They'd walked around the block, then cut down an alley and entered a hole-in-the-wall Italian restaurant through a back door. They now stood in a cramped storage room, the smells of fresh basil and oregano and ripe tomatoes wafting around them.

"It's all one-hundred percent legal," Mara said. "It's just that this is my side hustle and I don't want my corporate overlords to know about it."

Sy looked skeptical, but Austin said, "Then let's get to it."

"Alright, let's see what we've got here," Mara began. She reached into a large duffle bag, which she'd pulled out from behind a shelf filled with bags of flour. She handed Austin a black leather case.

"Wait," Sy said, "you keep high-end security equipment in a bag behind your flour shelf?"

"I keep it elsewhere. When you called, I had an associate bring it here. I own this place."

Sy frowned. "This is *wild.*"

In any other situation, Austin would have been just as uncomfortable. But he didn't see a lot of other options on the table.

"We can talk accommodations in a moment," Mara said, "but let's start with tools. Here we've got your basic burner laptop. It's a no-frills, stripped-down model. No bells and whistles, but what it lacks in features, it more than makes up for in anonymity. Fresh OS, full-disk encryption, and an anonymizing VPN pre-installed."

"This is all Greek to me," Austin said.

"You'll be *invisible*."

Sy cocked her head to the side with an approving look. "She knows what she's talking about."

Austin nodded. Since Sy had quite literally just given a talk on the subject of digital evidence gathering, he was glad she approved.

Next, Mara pulled out a slim, black device. "This is your phone. Not your average burner. It's been modified for multiple uses. Each call dynamically routed through a network of proxy servers to obscure your location. Prepaid, unregistered SIM, of course. Just don't get too attached, the key is to switch it out regularly. I included six extra SIMs. And the gas station burners you've been using—get rid of them." She shook her head. "Didn't you watch *The Wire*?"

Austin shrugged.

Mara sighed. "There's a whole plotline about how gas station burner phones can be tracked. Anyway, ditch them, this is better."

Austin took the phone, catching a look from Sy that he didn't want to think too hard about. She knew exactly how sketchy this all was and likely couldn't believe she was involved in it.

Reaching into a bag, Mara pulled out two small, sleek devices. "These are a couple of surplus tasers. Company models, top of the line, miniaturized. They've got a range of fifteen feet and can knock a guy out cold in two seconds. They were floor models, supposed to be junked, but let's just say they fell off the back of a truck."

"Now I *know* that's not legal," Sy interjected.

"Actually," Austin said, "in New York City tasers are legal, although they have to be registered."

"These *are* registered," Mara said, "to the company. Though if you end up using them or getting caught with them, well, it'll turn out they were stolen from the facility at which they were supposed to be destroyed. And you found it on the other guy, you get me?"

"When, in truth," Sy said, "*you* stole them from the people who employ you."

Mara put on a kind of pouty, little-girl face. "I already *know* Austin is carrying. Probably an unregistered firearm. Wouldn't you rather tase someone than shoot them?"

Austin looked at Sy, who nodded reluctantly. "I didn't know they came that small."

"These are top-of-the-line," Mara said.

"How much?" Austin asked. "For all of it."

Mara eyed all the equipment in Austin's arms as though calculating, but he didn't buy it. She'd known from the moment she walked in how much she wanted for it. "Ten thousand, plus whatever the hotel costs, probably three hundred a night plus my twenty-percent fee." She leaned back, looking from Sy to Austin and grinning conspiratorially. "One bed, or two?"

"Two," Sy said quickly. "We're just partners on this."

"Sure," Mara said. "Two beds it is. I don't do fake IDs, but this place doesn't require them. A pal of mine does it through his company so, well, it's a long story. But just check in under Mr. and Mrs. Jackson."

Austin nodded. "You'll text me the address on the new phone?"

"As long as I get my ten grand."

Austin said, "I'll send the first installment the minute we get to the hotel and I get online."

"The routing and account numbers are in the laptop. Search for a file called "Purple-haired goddess.""

Sy groaned. "Oh, please."

Mara gave Austin a side-eyed look. "I can see why you're not dating her." Then she grew serious. "I've never trusted anyone to walk out of my pizzeria without paying, but you're such a boy scout—well, I guess there's a first time for everything. Don't you dare try to screw me over, Austin. I know you know it wouldn't be difficult for me to track you down."

CHAPTER TWENTY

THE HOTEL WAS NICER than Austin had expected.

Nestled among the towering skyscrapers of the Financial District, it stood like a relic from another age. Its centuries-old brick facade was a stark contrast to the sleek glass and metal structures that dominated the neighborhood.

And as Austin led Sy through its heavy wooden doors, the bustling hum of the city faded behind them. It felt as though they were stepping into a different era.

Inside, the hotel exuded an air of historic charm. The lobby had a grand staircase with polished wooden banisters. Plush armchairs and antique tables filled the space, and rich mahogany wainscoting lined the walls. A crackling fireplace cast warm shadows over a worn but clean carpet. The only modern standout was a little café in the corner serving up 21st century drinks like oat milk lattes and keto-friendly protein muffins.

The check-in process went exactly as Mara had promised, and minutes later Austin was holding up the keycard to the sensor, another of the modern conveniences the hotel had adopted.

When he opened the door, he frowned. *This* was no suite.

And it certainly didn't have two beds. In fact, it was a room so small it could barely contain the one double bed in the corner.

"I think your pal may have charged us for a suite and pocketed the rest of the cash," Sy said.

"I'll take the floor," Austin said quickly.

"That's alright," Sy said. "You're taller than me, and older. And much more decrepit. Your back probably needs the bed."

"I'm not *that* much older," he said. "And my back is fine. I could never let you sleep on the floor." Austin set the bag of electronics on the small round table by the window. "Really. This is my fault. Let me take the floor."

Sy considered this. She looked like she was about to object, then her face broke out in a wide grin. "Done." She tossed two of the pillows on the floor next to the bed. "Welcome to your new home, Mr. Jackson."

An hour later, they'd managed to get the new laptop onto the wifi and Austin had wired money to Mara, as promised. He'd also sent the five names from Fiona's list to Samantha, asking her to look for any and all relevant information, such as criminal records, odd financial transactions and, of course, any connection to the Namgungs.

Next, Sy took over and ran a series of searches for Joey Green. Although they couldn't find the specifics of his departure from the Navy, they did find his prison record, which was just as good.

Turned out, Green served two years of a ten year sentence for possession of narcotics, with intent to distribute. His sentence had been commuted by the governor of New York, though they couldn't find any explanation to justify it.

What they *could* find were Green's social media accounts. "It's remarkable," Sy said, "how crooks go to such great lengths to conceal their crimes, then put all sorts of info online for anyone to see."

Austin scrolled through Green's Facebook account. "Far as I can tell, he doesn't seem to be a criminal anymore." Green was living his life out in the open now, proud of his sobriety and his new job: food services director on one of the ferries run by Statue Cruises, the company that ran tours for the Statue of Liberty. He never mentioned his time in prison, but few did when trying to build a new life.

"I know," Sy said, "but it's still remarkable how much people put out there. And this could all be a front, too. What it *does* do is make it easy for us to find him."

"You're thinking we try the boat?"

"You can take the sailor out of the Navy, but you can't take the sailor out of the sea," Sy said.

Austin looked at her, confused. "Is that a saying?"

She shrugged. "I just made it up."

"I feel like there's a better saying in there."

"My point is, it's interesting that he got canned by the Navy but ended up serving food on a different kind of boat."

Austin chuckled. "I've been on that boat. It's just nachos, popcorn and drinks. Makes the Navy food seem like Michelin-starred cuisine in comparison." He looked up the departure time of the next cruise. "Tomorrow, nine in the morning."

"I'm up for a ride. If we can get him to talk, we might be able to break this thing open by lunchtime."

Austin didn't think it was going to be that easy.

Sy took off her shoes and stretched out on the bed. "I think I saw a spare blanket in the closet."

"Thanks," Austin said. "I gotta make a call."

He took out the burner phone and called Kendall again. It had been too long since he'd spoken to her, and he was desperate for news. Pacing the hallway, he let it ring until it went to voicemail, then he called again.

And again. Nothing.

Standing at the door, he tried one more time. "Pick up pick up pick up," he whispered.

"Hello? Who is this?" It was Kendall's voice.

"Austin. New phone."

"I left you like four messages."

"I'm sorry. I had to ditch my other phones and... How's Run?"

"She's better. Still recovering. I got the full report and it was acute pancreatitis, like they initially thought. They'd hoped she'd just eaten something bad but, well, anyway. The surgery went well but they want to keep her there for another day or two. I had to go back to the office. Caught a case. But I'm on the phone with them and—"

"Can I have their number? I got a new phone and—"

Kendall gave him the number of the animal hospital which he typed into the contacts section of the phone.

"They're probably closed now," she said.

"But they have someone with her, right?"

"I'm sure they do."

Austin thanked her, hung up, and tried the number. The call went to voicemail and he left a message, requesting a call back.

When he tapped the keycard to get back into the room, Sy was snoring softly. She'd fallen asleep on top of the blankets, fully clothed.

Watching her, Austin realized how tired he was as well.

He found a spare blanket in the closet, took off his shoes, and lay on the floor. Despite his exhaustion, it took him a long time to get comfortable and even longer to fall asleep.

And it wasn't the floor that was keeping him up.

It was his thoughts.

They weren't racing. They were brooding.

Even though he was doing everything he could to solve Fiona's murder, it was as though a darkness had settled over him.

Like he expected to fail. Like he'd lost trust in himself, in his own judgment.

He bit his lip when another thought hit him. He expected Run to die. His rational mind told him she was fine. She was at the best animal hospital in the area and Kendall had just told him that she was healing well.

But he couldn't suppress the thought, no matter how hard he tried.

Dig two graves, Jorge had warned him.

And as sleep slowly came upon him all he could think about was how he'd failed Run like he failed Fiona. And now he was 3,000 miles away and there was nothing he could do to fix it.

Dig two graves.

Jorge's warning floated through his mind and moved through his dreams warning him that, despite his best efforts, that's exactly what he was doing.

He woke up with a start. He'd only been asleep for a few minutes.

In the dark, trying to get back to sleep on the hard floor, he found himself praying for the first time in years. Praying that he'd find The Magician and kill him, and that, if there had to be a second grave, it would be for himself, not Run.

CHAPTER TWENTY-ONE

JORGE JOLTED awake to the overpowering stench of rotting fish and saltwater. Where was he, and how long had he been out?

As his vision adjusted to the dim lighting, he realized he was bound to a chair in what appeared to be an old warehouse. Shafts of dawn light streamed through broken panes in the corrugated metal walls, illuminating swirling dust. The cries of seagulls echoed from somewhere outside.

Though the gag in his mouth distorted his senses, Jorge was almost certain he was somewhere along the Brooklyn shoreline. As a local of Manhattan Beach, he knew the fishing industries that once thrived here had shut down years ago. He wondered if this musty warehouse was one of the relics from that era. He already knew that Javier had been killed in a Manhattan beach pizzeria. No doubt the gang had a few warehouses as well.

Squinting as his eyes adjusted, Jorge could barely make out a faded stencil on the wall that read "Brooklyn Seafood Packers."

Maria and the children. As he thought of them he was hit with a sudden, violent rage. And a desire to escape.

He struggled against the ropes binding him to the chair, but it was no use. All he did was tip over the chair and crash himself to the floor, striking his cheek on the cold concrete.

His heart pounded as he heard approaching footsteps, then saw two masked men emerge from the shadows.

The two men were the same height but one was older, slightly built, and wore an ill-fitting black suit that hung loosely off his thin frame. The other was a barrel of a man—somewhere between fat and muscular—and wore only a tight black t-shirt and jeans. He didn't recognize them, but he knew why they were there.

The slight man held a cellphone, the larger man held a base-ball bat wrapped in barbed wire. The slight man tapped his phone and the camera light flashed on, reflecting the damp floors and dusty crates. "Pick him up."

The other lay down his bat and hurried over to set Jorge's chair upright, lifting both Jorge and the chair like he was picking up a small puppy curled up in a doggy bed.

The slight man raised the phone to Jorge's face. "It's time," he said. "Time to speak." He stepped forward and pulled the gag out of Jorge's mouth.

Jorge opened his mouth wide, stretching out his stiff jaw. "What do you want? Who are you?" He'd told himself he would say nothing, admit nothing, give them nothing. But he couldn't help himself.

The man with the bat leapt forward and swung wildly, a terrible gleam in his eyes as he brought it down on the floor a few inches from Jorge's foot. The barbed wire scraped against the floor like a fork on a chalkboard.

"We will tell you what to say," the slight man said. "You will say it or he will hit you with his bat." He had a slight accent Jorge could not place. Possibly Chilean, he thought, but the man had a look about him that was more Northern European. Blond hair, blue eyes and pale, creamy skin.

Jorge closed his eyes. There was no way he was going to make a hostage video for these bastards.

He heard the man's voice again. "You will say to the husband, 'Come in and give yourself up and they will let me go.'"

The husband. Austin, they were talking about Thomas Austin. That told Jorge that they knew they could deal with everyone else, or perhaps they already had. Murdered, bribed, or otherwise silenced. But Austin was the one they were most worried about.

Jorge shook his head.

What happened next happened all at once, but later Jorge could remember it as though it had happened in slow motion. First he heard a half-second whoosh of air, then the bat struck his leg, crushing down on his thigh and gashing it with razor sharp wire.

He screamed in pain and tipped to the left, toppling over again and hitting his head on the floor. Just as quickly, the man with the bat lifted the chair back upright and struck his other leg, knocking him to the right. This time, he kept his head high enough to keep it from hitting the floor, but he could feel the blood trickling from the wounds on his legs.

The slight man approached Jorge and crouched down to meet his eyes. "All we want is for you to say a few things to your friend. He's the last piece of this we need cleaned up."

Jorge held his pale blue eyes and shook his head again. "The last piece? What about Voohrees, Baker, and Palini?"

The man gave him a quizzical look. "Oh, they were sent out with the trash a long time ago. We don't always send videos." He stood and stepped back, then nodded at the man with the bat, giving him permission to strike again.

Cocking the bat over his head, he stepped toward Jorge, then paused and spoke for the first time, words clipped and running together with that classic New York rhythm. "Do you like pain, señor?"

CHAPTER TWENTY-TWO

SY WAS ALREADY UP and making coffee. The light streamed in through the crack in the curtains and, for a fraction of a moment, Austin was happy. He wasn't sure what it was... something about the fall light in the city that he'd always loved.

But the feeling quickly dissipated when he remembered where he was, and why.

"Coffee?" Sy asked. "They've got one of those pod thingies."

"Please," Austin said, sitting up and reaching for the phone he'd gotten from Mara.

Sy handed him a cup. "Black, right?"

Austin nodded. "Thanks." The first sip was only halfway down his throat when he thought of Run. Taking another big sip and sucking in air to try to avoid burning his mouth, he grabbed the burner laptop and logged onto Facebook. Mara had assured him that, though it was theoretically possible to be tracked through Facebook, someone would need to hack into Facebook servers to find his IP address, then fight through dozens of re-directs and anonymity filters. So, unless they happened to have someone on the payroll at Facebook, it wasn't likely.

He had a new message from Kendall. A photo.

It was Kendall, wearing a black leather jacket and looking as stylish as ever, except for one major difference. Run was sitting in her lap, licking her face. Her torso was wrapped in a white bandage, but she looked every bit the happy pup he'd left behind.

Under the photo was a message.

She's fine. Another half day in the hospital and I'll check her out, then I won't leave her alone until you get back. Only thing is I'll have to keep her away from Ralph so she doesn't run so hard her stitches come out.

Austin smiled and sipped his coffee, staring at the photo. It was the only good news he'd gotten in quite some time.

As he was about to close his laptop, another little red "1" appeared on his messages on Facebook.

He opened it and saw that it was from "Sarah Davidson," a name he didn't know. He clicked over to her profile and saw that it had been created only one day earlier. Almost certainly a fake account.

His stomach twisted when he returned to the message and saw that it was a video. Jorge, bruised and bloodied, had been tied to a chair that was tipped over, his face bleeding out onto a concrete floor.

He was alive, but breathing slowly.

A hand came in from the left of the shot holding up a copy of *The New York Post*. The date was circled. It was from this morning. The video had been taken in the last couple hours. They'd probably sent it to his cellphone and email as well.

As horrifying as it was, Austin was relieved that Jorge was alive at all.

As the camera zoomed in on Jorge's face, a voice came from off screen. "This is your friend. We would like to let him live but that will be up to you. If you receive this message, reply with a simple 'OK.' Our next message will tell you where to meet."

"What is it?" Sy asked, sitting next to him and holding a cup of coffee.

"It's bad." Austin played her the video.

When it was over, Sy played it again. "That's Jorge, right? The man you thought was having an affair with Fiona?"

"Yeah, and it turned out he was working closely with her on the case. His theory was that they only let him live because he was lower than her, didn't know as much. I think they know I'm onto something."

Sy suddenly grew serious and closed the laptop. "I'm gonna bet I'm thinking more clearly than you right now, so here's the deal. First, you're not going to meet them. It will not help Jorge and it won't help you. They'll just kill you both."

Austin didn't reply. He knew she was probably right, but the thought of Jorge being tortured made him want to do something, anything, even if that meant walking into a trap that would almost certainly prove deadly.

"Next," Sy continued, "you need to send that video to the NYPD and the FBI. They are out looking for Jorge and I'm certain that's a better clue than anything they have."

"I know," he said.

"Now."

He was already on it. He saved the video to the desktop, then sent it through the anonymous tip email addresses to both the NYPD and the New York branch of the FBI. He copied the message as well, and added an explanation of how he'd gotten it.

It was a long shot, but maybe the man's voice would be recognized by someone, or perhaps some detail of the location might trigger something in them that it hadn't in Austin.

"Good," Sy said when he'd finished.

"And this is the hardest part," she said, touching his leg. "You have to forget about the video. We need to keep going with the plan. Joey Green. The names on that list."

"But—"

"No, listen. If they give you a location and you show up, there is not any chance you show up there and live. Got it? And there's not any chance that Jorge lives if you show up on your own. You two might be the last pieces of this, and they won't kill *him* as long as *you're* out of their reach. You show up and they have no reason to keep him alive."

Austin considered this. "Maybe, but—"

"But nothing. You know I'm right. It's just your hero complex that makes you think you should show up and try to save the day." She stood. "I'm gonna use the bathroom, then we're going to find Joey Green. Maybe he can give us something to find The Magician. That's our best bet to get Jorge out alive."

CHAPTER TWENTY-THREE

THE SUV HAD BEEN WAITING for them. Bright silver with dark tinted windows, Austin noticed it idling as he stepped out of the hotel. His first thought was that it was the people who'd found him before, at his previous hotel in Manhattan Beach.

But these folks didn't appear to be killers, and they didn't appear to be trying to conceal the fact that they were waiting for him. In fact, as Sy tried to hail a taxi, a tall woman with perfectly-neat dreadlocks got out of the passenger seat and walked right up to Austin. "I'm Deborah Owimikea, deputy chief of staff to Mayor McKinley. She'd like to speak with you and your associate."

Deborah wore a bright white skirt suit with a striking, double-breasted blazer anointed with gold buttons.

Austin thought fast. Assuming Mara's laptop was as secure as she'd promised, there was no way they'd been traced already. And their names were nowhere on the hotel reservation.

"How'd you know where we were staying?" he asked, taking a step back.

The woman tossed her hair back. "It's nothing nefarious, Mr. Austin. It has come to the mayor's attention that you are in her city investigating a murder and, well, our facial recognition software placed you at this hotel. Perfectly legal."

Sy had come to stand next to Austin. "Maybe the mayor can help," she offered.

What she didn't mention was that Mayor McKinley was one of the five names on Fiona's list. Austin was quite sure she knew that as well as he did, and this was her way of telling him that they should go.

"Would the meeting be at the mayor's office?" Austin asked.

Deborah nodded. "Of course." She walked back to the SUV and opened the door to the back seat. "It'll just take a few minutes."

"Do we have a choice?" Austin asked.

She laughed. "Of *course* you do. But not a lot of people get to meet with her one on one. It's an honor for you."

Austin almost laughed. But he had to admit, he'd already decided to go. After all, of the five people on Fiona's list, she was perhaps best positioned to manipulate the drug trade within New York City. Plus, Sy was already on her way to the SUV.

"Please have a seat," Deborah said, smoothing an invisible crease in her blazer. "The mayor will be right with you."

Sy sat next to Austin on a sofa that wasn't as nice as he would have expected in a mayor's waiting room. Its cushions were worn thin and the pillows needed restuffing.

Sy made eye contact with Austin and nodded as though she was trying to communicate with him telepathically. His guess was that she was wondering what he was wondering: how should they approach questioning the mayor?

What he hoped was that she was coming to the same conclusion he'd come to: Let the mayor lead the way. No good could come from accusing her of anything and, after all, she'd asked them for a meeting, not the other way around.

"Thomas Austin? Is that you?" It was a man's voice from the doorway.

Austin looked up.

"Whoa! I *thought* that was you."

Austin studied his face for a moment, then recognition swept over him. "Amelio?" Austin stood and greeted his warm smile with one of his own. "Good to see you."

Amelio shook his hand eagerly. "What the heck are you doing here?"

Sy stood and cleared her throat.

Austin stepped back. "Oh, sorry, Sy. This is Amelio Sullivan. Deputy Mayor and former DA. Fiona worked with him way back in the day and we played cards a couple times at charity poker nights for the families of fallen officers. Amelio, this is Symone Aoki. NCIS." He didn't mention her suspension, and he also didn't mention that Fiona had dated Amelio in law school.

Amelio shook his head in mock sadness. "I still remember that time Fiona called my bluff and took me for six-hundred bucks. But it was for charity, so..."

Austin laughed. "I think it was eight hundred."

"Good to meet you," Sy said.

They'd dated before Austin and Fiona had even met and Fiona had never given him any reason to be jealous. Still, Amelio had the looks of a model—high cheekbones, a strong jawline, and a bald head that he pulled off better than anyone Austin had ever known. Not to mention he had the career-trajectory of a rocket ship. Fiona had often called him "the one good politician," and his rise through the ranks gave Austin some faith that not all politicians were to be regarded with suspicion.

"So what the heck are you doing back in NYC?" Amelio asked. "Back to rejoin the NYPD, I hope. The department would be stronger with you in it."

"Nah," Austin said. "I'm here looking into a case."

"And you're meeting with *her*?" Amelio asked, nodding toward the door to the mayor's office. "Good luck."

He leaned in close and whispered in Austin's ear. "She'll probably give you nothing, but if I can do anything to help, lemme know." He leaned back and slid a business card into the breast pocket of Austin's shirt.

"Look, I've gotta get to a meeting." He reached out and shook Austin's hand, then Sy's. "Great to meet you," he said to Sy. "And Austin, good to see you, too. Seriously, think about coming back. We could get you back on the force in a matter of weeks."

The mayor's office was decorated with many photos, mostly of herself. She was in her mid-fifties and, in addition to solo shots of the silver-haired New Yorker, there were plenty of shots of her posing with dignitaries from the president of Chad to the New York Governor to multiple U.S. Presidents. She certainly didn't want to hide the fact that she was on a first-name basis with many important people.

As he stared at her, waiting for her to look up from her phone, he couldn't help but wonder whether she had the clout to get the governor of New York to commute the sentence of a convicted felon like Joey Green. She probably did. And if she'd done that, what else might she have done?

"You know," Mayor McKinley said, finally setting her phone down on the desk, "your wife once called me an elitist at a mixer."

Austin's mouth dropped open.

"But some of us," she continued, "have earned the right to be elitist because we are, in fact, elite."

She looked from Austin to Sy, her tight, botoxed face betrayed nothing.

Finally, she let out a thin, cruel laugh. "Oh I'm only joking. She did call me *elitist* though." She sighed. "And maybe she was right. But I can't help the fact that I was raised on the Upper West Side and attended the finest schools."

"Why'd you call us in here?" Austin asked.

"I'll answer your question with one of my own: why are you in New York?"

Austin knew there was no point in lying. The article about Fiona would have gotten back to her, and, even if she wasn't The Magician, surely she was staying abreast of developments through the NYPD. "Looking into my wife's murder. A murder your police department has failed to solve."

She narrowed her eyes on him. "A murder *you* failed to solve as well, before you tucked your tail between your legs and disappeared."

Austin felt the anger burning in his chest, but he said nothing. The truth was, she was right. After taking four bullets in the shooting that had killed his wife, Austin had tried to rejoin the NYPD, but he'd been too damaged, too on-edge, to do any good.

Soon after, he resigned and moved west.

Deborah, who was standing by the door, cleared her throat. "You have WNYC in five minutes, ma'am."

"I'm running behind," Mayor McKinley said, "but I need to tell you something. I know Fiona never liked me, and you probably don't either. But trust me when I tell you, you're not going to do any good here. Really. There's a lot going on you don't know about. You need to leave New York."

"I'll leave after Fiona's killers have been caught, or I'll leave in a casket." Austin heard the words coming out of his mouth before he'd decided to say them.

Mayor McKinley flashed her dark blue eyes at him, then shook her head. "What a cowboy. Let me be perfectly frank. You two have absolutely no standing poking around this investigation." She moved her glare from Austin to Sy, then back to Austin. "An NCIS agent from Connecticut and a PI licensed in Washington State? You have no authority here. Like it or not, this is *my* city. This matter is leagues above your capabilities and clearances. The NYPD and FBI have jurisdiction, not some naval interloper and off-brand gumshoe."

She let her gaze sweep up and down Austin's wrinkled clothes, which he'd now been wearing for at least three days. He could almost taste her disdain for him.

"There are exceedingly sensitive operations at play," she continued, "and I'll not have them jeopardized by your meddling. However well-intentioned your vigilante fancies may be, you are out of your depth. You risk fouling up the efforts of *proper* authorities, who—quite frankly—do not need distractions from rank amateurs."

She stood and leaned across her vast desk. "I strongly advise you to leave this be. We have enough real issues to deal with without you intermeddlers fouling things up."

"Intermeddlers?" Sy asked. It was the first word she'd spoken, and her tone had both mirth and anger in it. "Is that what you said?"

"You heard me," Mayor McKinley said.

"Oh, I could hear you. I just wanted to make sure *you* could hear you."

McKinley smiled a cold, bitter smile. "There are things at work here beyond your purview. So do be good chaps and toddle off back to your rightful places. Leave the investigating to my NYPD. Am I quite clear?" She didn't wait for an answer. With a dismissive wave, she said, "Splendid."

As if summoned by a genie, Deborah appeared at Austin's elbow and ushered them out of the room.

"Gee," Sy said in the elevator, "I wonder what could have *possibly* given Fiona the idea that she's elitist."

CHAPTER TWENTY-FOUR

THE FERRY to the Statue of Liberty bore little resemblance to the ferries back in Washington State. This was no utilitarian workhorse plying the waters of Puget Sound loaded with commuters and tourists, cars and bikes. This was a sleek, specialized passenger craft with a sole purpose: transporting visitors to and from Lady Liberty.

Austin brushed his hair out of his eyes as the wind whipped off the water with an intensity he'd never felt on the ferries that traversed the Puget Sound. Standing on the exposed deck, the wind also cut through his jacket and blew it like a flag in a storm. Behind him, the city skyline receded. Ahead, the Statue of Liberty rose green and grand against the vivid blue sky, a stirring sight.

As he followed Sy into the cabin, he noticed that the general tone of the passengers on the ferry differed, too. The Washington ferries were quiet except on Seahawks or Mariners game days. Most often people read, sipped coffee, scrolled on their phones, worked on laptops, or chatted in small groups. This boat buzzed with the spirited chatter of giddy tourists.

Sy stopped suddenly, pointing toward a little booth with a line leading toward it. "That's him. That's Joey Green."

"C'mon," Austin said. "I'll buy you a hot dog."

Through their online research, they'd put together a decent picture of Joey Green. From what they could tell, he was about as New Jersey as it got. Though he didn't share anything about his past on social media, he posted video after video in which he shared strong opinions about New Jersey and New York sports teams, making Austin think poor Joey had missed his calling as a sports radio host. They'd also learned that he had a daughter named Becca. He became a father when he was only eighteen.

Green was in his early thirties, with a compact, muscular build and tightly wound presence, though his face had a droopy look that suggested late nights or early mornings. Perhaps both. And his eyes betrayed a lot, darting from nacho cheese to soda to customers in an almost paranoid manner.

Standing three back in the line as he dished up nachos and pretzels for tourists, Austin recognized the tattoo on his forearm: a flaming skull wearing a Navy cap.

When they reached the front of the line, Austin let the one person behind them go ahead. When the person left with their bottled water, Austin put his hands on the counter. "Two hot dogs, please."

Green eyed him, probably wondering why he'd let someone go in front of him. Then he returned and got the hot dogs. "Ten bucks even."

"Hey, aren't you Joey Green," Sy said. "I recognize you from Facebook. Go Devils, right?"

Green smiled a yellow-toothed, crooked-teeth smile. "They're looking good this year. If they can find a goalkeeper who knows what the hell he's doing, maybe we can go somewhere."

Austin paid for the hot dogs. "Hey, there's something else, though."

He'd been contemplating how to approach Joey for the last ten minutes. He could tell they weren't going to deceive him into revealing anything about his past, so he decided to come right out with it. "Your name came up in a case I'm working on. I'm a private investigator. Thomas Austin."

He held out his hand to shake but Joey stepped back, eyes darting from Austin to Sy, then back to Austin.

"Anyway, you've done nothing wrong," Austin continued, trying to put as much reassurance into his voice as he could. "My case has little or nothing to do with you. Just following up on some stuff about the USS Sea Prowler."

Joey folded his arms, tightening his forearm then relaxing it over and over, which made it look like the flaming skull in the Navy cap was bulging and shrinking as though it were truly on fire.

"So, the case I'm looking into has to do with a big drug smuggling ring. Lotta higher-ups. Southeast Asia. Maybe the Namgungs." With each word Austin watched Joey's eyes, looking for a flash, a flinch, something.

But he got nothing. Just a hard, New-Jersey scowl.

"I know you're clean as a whistle now," Austin offered. He could feel Joey Green's resolve hardening. "Trust me. But back in the day, well, we were wondering if maybe you could tell us anything about some of the stuff that was happening on the sub back then. Maybe tell us if anyone else might be involved. Higher ups in the Navy, maybe some politicians or..."

He wasn't sure, but Austin thought his eyes might have frozen temporarily on the word *politicians*.

He glanced at Sy, who had seen it, too. "Politicians," Sy said. "Buncha crooks, if you ask me. Always trying to make the little guy do the *hard time* when they make all the real money. Am I right, Joey?"

Suddenly, something was wrong, but Austin didn't know what. The ferry had slowed, gone quiet.

"We're drifting," Sy said. She looked to Joey. "What happened?"

"Been having trouble with the vessel," Joey said, his voice guarded. "Engine kicks off sometimes. They'll get it fixed up."

Though they were close to their destination, the ferry was drifting slowly, silently, no longer chugging along.

Austin folded his arms. "You say this happens a lot?"

"Just in the last week." Joey turned around and loaded a new batch of popcorn kernels into the metal popper hooked to the top of a large glass popcorn case. "Engine issue. They're looking into it. Supposedly." He started the machine, which gave a low roar as the heater kicked on. "Makes no difference to me. Way I see it, the longer they ride, the hungrier they get. We'll sell a few extra dogs this trip. And popcorn."

Austin decided that he wasn't lying, at least not about the ship's engine trouble. "Good, that'll give us more time to talk, too."

"I can't say much about the past. But ask me anything and, if I can, I'll answer."

"Well, we just want to know who else might be involved," Austin said.

Just as the kernels began to explode, Joey used two hands to vault himself over the counter, knocking over a small candy bar display. At a full sprint, he busted through the glass door onto the deck.

"Where the hell does he think he's going?" Austin asked, taken aback.

"He's not rational," Sy said. "That dude is a caged animal. Caged by his past, and by fear. At least he was nice enough to put on a batch of popcorn for us."

Austin moved to the door. "Even so, he's not getting away."

CHAPTER TWENTY-FIVE

AUSTIN SPOTTED Joey through the crowd lining the side of the vessel. With a jolt of adrenaline, he bolted, weaving through the throng of sightseers. His shoes clanged on the metal decking as he rounded the side of the ferry, the salty sea air mingling with the taste of cold metal—like biting down on a nickel—which his synesthesia always delivered in times like this.

Following Joey, he bounded up the stairs two at a time, reaching the top deck. The wind whipped through his hair, carrying with it the distant sounds of laughter and chatter from below, punctuated by the occasional squawk of a seagull overhead.

They were probably only a quarter mile from the Statue of Liberty, which rose up behind Joey against the clear October sky, her torch held high.

Backlit by the early afternoon sun, Joey stood at the edge of the deck, leaning against a hard plastic wall.

"Joey, I just want to talk," Austin called out, his voice fighting against the wind.

Joey turned slowly, his arms spread wide in a show of mock innocence. A giant Herring Gull flew down and started pecking at the ground near them. Austin took another step forward, his eyes locked on Joey's.

"You served your time," Austin said. "I'm not an officer. I have zero authority here. Really. I just want to talk."

"Fine," Joey said, which caught Austin by surprise. "Fine, I'll talk. Just didn't want to talk in front of that broad. She made me nervous. Not a big fan of her type."

"Her type?" That caught Austin off guard. His training told him just to keep Joey talking. The more comfortable the witness, the more he'd be likely to say. At the same time, this guy was really starting to piss him off.

Austin stepped toward him and, in the blink of an eye, Joey's foot shot out, tripping Austin at the ankle. The gull flew off to avoid the commotion. Before Austin knew what was happening, Joey was yanking him up with surprising strength. Austin flailed, his arms striking the low wall separating the upper deck from the air.

Joey shoved him up against the wall. Austin swung his head forward, striking Joey on the nose. Blood sprayed Austin's face, obscuring his vision. But the blow didn't seem to phase Joey because the next thing Austin knew, he was falling. Joey had half lifted, half shoved him over the wall.

The world spun as he crashed onto the deck one level below. The impact jarred his shoulder and his head smacked against the hard surface.

His vision blurred and his senses were filled with the metallic tang of his own blood, the harsh cries of gulls, and the distant murmur of the city.

The bright October day suddenly seemed much colder as darkness began to creep in around the edges of his vision. This, Austin knew, was what a concussion felt like.

CHAPTER TWENTY-SIX

SY SPIED Joey hurrying down the steps and stayed just far enough behind him to follow him without being noticed. But it was a small ferry and neither of them could avoid the other for long.

But where the hell was Austin? She thought he'd chased Joey to the upper deck, but when she'd made it to the stairs leading up, she'd seen Joey descending.

There was no time to figure that out. Joey hurried around the front of the ship, then ducked through a door. A wooden plaque out front read "Security."

Swallowing hard, Sy followed him in.

"Get her out of here," Joey barked. "She's harassing me. Following me." He'd already made it to the corner of the little room and a couple security guards in yellow vests stood near the door, looking surprised to see her.

Thinking fast, she pulled out her badge. "Symone Aoki, NCIS."

Austin had tried to play it nice. She was going to try a different route.

The security guards stepped back, deferring instinctively to the badge. They didn't need to know she was suspended.

"Here's the thing, Joey. I—"

"Can't you guys kick her out or something?" Joey pleaded with the guards. "I work here. I—"

The engine suddenly roared to life and a few cheers erupted from outside. Slowly, the ferry resumed its course for the island.

Everyone in the security office ignored this.

"Here's what I know about you Joey. You're a former high school athlete. You joined the Navy, probably because you believe in serving your country and also you didn't have many other options. My hunch is that you were already dealing when you joined the Navy. Nothing serious, maybe just a few pain pills, amphetamines, that kind of thing."

He raised his hands up to object, but Sy silenced him with a look.

"But here's the thing. Sometime in the mid-teens, someone approached you. Maybe they had something on you. Maybe they used your young daughter against you."

His eyes flashed.

"Yeah, I know about Becca. The way you brag about her on Facebook, I can tell how much you love her."

"Leave her out of this," Joey said.

"I'm sorry, but I can't do that. You see, I need to figure out how they got you to help them. It's my job to do that. And just like you'd do anything to protect her, I'll do anything to *do my job* because it's that important to *me*."

∽

Where the hell was he?

Austin sat up, blinking slowly and reaching instinctively for his shoulder, which was numb.

A young man was crouching next to him. "Are you okay?" The man asked. I'm a med student and... I saw it all. You fell on your shoulder, luckily, or you would have broken your neck."

He rubbed his shoulder and tried to move it. "I can't feel anything there. I'm more worried about my head." He tried to stand, but wobbled when he tried to press himself up, then sat down cross-legged.

The med student put a hand on Austin's knee. "You likely have a concussion. If your shoulder is numb after a fall like that, it's not something to take lightly. A bunch of things could be going on." He gestured to his own shoulder, using it as a visual aid. "You've got a ton of nerves running through this area, right? If you've injured one of those, it might cause numbness or tingling. If a nerve got stretched too far or pinched when you fell, it could be messing with the signals it sends to your brain. Now, if you've dislocated your shoulder, that's when the bone in your upper arm gets popped out of the socket, it could also cause numbness, especially if the dislocation is pressing on a nerve."

Austin let the kid talk—he seemed to be enjoying himself—but as he listened he scanned the deck. A small crowd had gathered around them, some looking at him, some filming him with their phones, some looking up toward the upper deck roughly twelve feet above.

He didn't see Sy or Joey.

The med student leaned back, crossing his arms thoughtfully. "And then there's the possibility of a fracture. If you broke a bone and it's pressing on a nerve, that could be causing the numbness. But again, you'd normally feel a lot of pain with a fracture. I might just be a medical student, but that's not something you want to mess around with."

"Thanks," Austin said. "It's not a fracture. I can tell." He wasn't sure of that, but he hadn't heard a crack, and that was good enough for him. "I'm gonna walk it off."

He pressed himself up, putting both feet on the ground and standing slowly. After holding onto the railing for a few seconds and ignoring the med student's advice, he wandered around toward the front of the ferry.

Sy couldn't have gone far.

CHAPTER TWENTY-SEVEN

AUSTIN HAD LOOKED EVERYWHERE ELSE on the ferry by the time he poked his head into the security office. Sy stood in front of Joey in the corner, but before he could get a word out, a large security guard stepped out to greet him, pushing him out of the doorway.

"You can't go in there," the guard said. "Meeting in progress."

"I'm with the lady in there."

"You NCIS, too?"

"Sort of," Austin lied.

"Badge?"

"That guy in there just shoved me over the railing of the second deck."

The guard stepped back, eyed him. "You look fine."

His head had cleared slightly and the numbness in his shoulder had disappeared, replaced now by a low throbbing accentuated by pinpricks of pain. "Attempted murder is still attempted murder, even if the attempt fails."

"Look, Mr., I'm a security guard on a tourist ferry making twenty-two bucks an hour. Do you know how far twenty-two bucks an hour gets me in New York City?"

"Not far?"

"It gets me a couch in the living room in a two-bedroom apartment with five other people. That lady in there had a real badge. And I notice she's not rushing out to vouch for you. Show me one and I'll let you in, otherwise, go to hell."

Austin backed off. The man had a point. Why wasn't Sy rushing out to vouch for him? Most likely it was because she thought she could have better luck getting Joey to talk without him there.

Reluctantly, he turned to go.

Finding a bench on the side of the ferry, he checked his cellphone, which, thankfully, hadn't been damaged by the fall. If Sy was going to handle the interview, maybe he could make progress on another aspect of the investigation. He dialed Samantha, who picked up immediately.

"I was hoping you'd call me," she said. "I've got some news on your list."

Even through the phone, Austin could hear the familiar sound of rain pattering a window, a contrast to the bright, sunny day he was experiencing. "That's great," Austin said.

"Chief Justice Evelyn Lim. Cardinal James Dellacorte. Far as we can tell, there are good explanations for what you found."

"Hit me."

"Justice Evelyn Lim. Given her position, she's got numerous cases and litigations that she oversees. That's normal, and the fact that some involve drug cases or city officials, also normal. She's been more lenient than some other Justices might have been, but she's a liberal Justice. She's pretty lenient in general, not just in drug cases."

"Okay, but—"

"We *also* did a deep-dive into her finances and she shows no signs of corruption. *Follow the money*, as the saying goes. Wasn't hard because we've been looking at campaign contributions and corruption anyway, so we know what it looks like. She's broke. Well, not broke, but as broke as a judge can be. I mean, she makes $250,000 a year. But in New York, as a sixty-year-old divorcee with two kids in grad school, that's actually not that much. She wrote a book, but it didn't sell. She doesn't appear to have any extra money."

"Interesting," Austin said, as the ferry began to dock.

"And Cardinal James Dellacorte. With him we started by looking at his personal finances. Not as broke as a cardinal ought to be, but nothing egregious."

"Where does the extra money come from?"

"That's the thing. He's gotten some large, unexplained donations, which were sketchy as hell, but it turns out they came from wire transfers from Barbados, and they have nothing to do with the Namgungs, or the FBI or the NYPD or New York State."

"So where *do* they come from?"

"You ever heard of Talus Aaron Ockley?"

"Is he that space guy?"

"Yeah, among other things he's the owner of BlueSpace Horizon Industries, a commercial space flight venture that wants to colonize mars by 2045. Anyway, he's a Catholic. He donates millions to all sorts of causes, all anonymously."

"Then how'd you find out?"

Samantha laughed. "Well, not anonymously to *me*. Bottom line, he's donated money to Dellacorte. Far as I can tell, zero connection to the Namgungs. Quite frankly, the kind of billions that Ockley makes through technology are so far beyond what an organization like the Namgungs brings in. There's just nothing there."

"Thanks, anything else?" Austin asked.

"Well, with all five of those people, there is a firehouse of disinformation out there. Part of that is just how the internet works these days, but with those five it's next level. It's very possible Fiona got some bad info. How sure are you that it's one of the five people on that list?"

Sy was at the end of her rope. She'd tried threats, lies, and promises, and now the ferry was about to dock. Joey knew as well as she did that she had no right to hold him there.

So she decided to go with something she only tried in the rarest of circumstances. Her heart. "Joey, you know you don't have to talk to me. Sure I've got this badge, but you know it doesn't mean much."

She looked from one of the guards to the other, then back at Joey, who sat with his arms folded, a scowl across his face.

"I'm going to tell you a story. I read about it in the paper a few weeks ago and I didn't believe it so I called one of the officers on duty and asked if it had really happened. It had. It's a story about a two year old girl in the Bronx. Her mom was a single mom and dropped her off at the same daycare from 9:00 to 4:00 every day while she went to work. The little girl was smart and funny and charismatic and was already learning how to dance. Her mom put the videos on YouTube for her relatives to watch."

Sy crouched in front of Joey and met his eyes. "Police were called to the daycare when the girl was found unresponsive, lying in the corner next to a pile of Legos. Turned out she had eaten a little pill she found on the floor. Fentanyl. It destroyed her from the inside. Killed her within ten minutes."

Sy struck the floor with an open palm, jolting Joey from his chair. "A two-year-old girl dead from fentanyl in the Bronx while her mom worked at the Jamaican pie shop six doors down. Do you know how those drugs got into New York City, into that daycare? Because *I* damn well do and I think you do, too. One of the staff members was an addict and it had fallen out of his pocket. Before that, a container from Southeast Asia, a drug mule from Columbia, maybe. Doesn't matter how exactly, but it was someone like the man you used to be who brought it in."

She closed her eyes, lowered her voice. "I also know you've got a girl of your own, a teenager. And I know that you no longer do the things that bring those drugs into New York City, but we both know you once did. Didn't you?"

She opened her eyes again and, to her surprise, Joey was openly crying.

"This is one of those moments, Joey. One of the moments you'll think back on when you're sixty, seventy years old. You'll either be thinking about it with regret while getting blackout drunk because you can't deal with the pain you've caused yourself by hurting others, or you'll be thinking about it with a bittersweet tenderness because, for once, you chose to do the right thing. Because it was a turning point in your life."

There was a long silence, then Joey said. "We're docked and I've gotta shut down the food stand. Boat heads back in an hour. Get off the ferry and I'll meet you in ten minutes."

CHAPTER TWENTY-EIGHT

SY EXPLAINED the situation to Austin as they followed the crowd streaming off of the ferry. Instead of continuing down the walkway toward the statue with the throng of tourists, they found a spot on a bench and waited.

After ten minutes, during which Austin filled her in on his call with Samantha, Austin asked, "You sure he's not blowing you off?"

"Sure? No. But I don't think he is. I actually think he's a decent guy."

Austin rubbed his shoulder. The sharp pain had turned into a throbbing, agonizing ache, but he was fairly sure it wasn't broken. "He pushed me over the railing."

"He was scared, that's my guess."

"Went a little overboard, don't you think? No pun intended."

Sy shrugged. "Oh, you're fine."

"Easy for you to say. You're not the one who—"

She pointed. "There."

Joey was wandering toward them, sucking on a vape pen and blowing a stream of pale gray mist off to his side.

Austin stood as he approached. If Sy was right and he was

ready to talk, the last thing he wanted was to scare him off. "No hard feelings," he said as Joey neared. "And I'll leave if you only want to talk to Sy."

Joey glanced at Sy, then shook his head and looked back at Austin. "Earlier, I said I didn't like her type. That was BS. My girl's mama was from South Korea. Still is, actually. She left me and, well, I've been pissed ever since. Ms. Aoki reminded me of her and..." he shook his head back and forth violently, then took another hit of nicotine from his vape pen... "can't get my head on right these days. I say weird shit sometimes."

"All is forgiven," Sy said, trying to move on as quickly as possible from his strange, tangled admission. "Have a seat."

Joey passed his vape pen from hand to hand nervously. "What I'm about to tell you could get me killed. It's why I ran, why I pushed you over the side." He closed his eyes tight. "I got a video this morning."

"Was it a man named Jorge tied to a chair?" Austin asked. "Copy of the newspaper with today's date circled?"

Joey looked up. "How'd you know?"

Sy said, "Because we got it, too. The people behind this are dangerous. They are cleaning house. My hunch, Joey, is that you've covered for them in the past. And they want to make sure you're still going to stay quiet."

He nodded. "That's right."

"They'd reward you handsomely if you told them where I am," Austin said. "You call them right now and tell them where I am, they'll owe you big time."

Joey's eyes got wide, and he seemed to be considering it.

Austin waited until he turned to look at him, then said, "I'm telling you this because I need you to trust me, Joey."

Joey's face was neutral. "I don't trust anyone."

"But still, you're not going to call them, are you?"

Joey looked at the ground. "That's the thing. There is no 'them.' I was small time. I don't even know who 'them' *is*."

"Then tell us what you *do* know," Sy said.

As the wind blew gently through the trees overhead and the tourists snapped photos of the Statue of Liberty a few hundred yards away, Joey told his story. "I'm a pretty simple guy. Jersey through and through. Half Italian, half Jewish. Grew up thinking I'd play for the Devils, and if not them, the Yankees." He laughed, shaking his head. "Stupid kid! Shortstop for the Yankees was my *fallback* if I wasn't good enough to play pro hockey.

"Long story short, I was okay in high school but wasn't good enough to make my junior college team. Freshman year I got into pain pills, first for actual pain, then for fun. So I joined the Navy, a cook, a Navy cook, but that barely paid the bills. Not like NHL money, right? So I got into some extracurricular activities. Nothing hardcore at first, just playing delivery boy for some recreational pharmaceuticals.

"But one thing led to another and I got busted by the local cops. Thought my goose was cooked. But then the feds show up with an offer I couldn't refuse. They wanted me to snitch in exchange for a suspended sentence. Said there was something going on in the Navy and could I hang around and see what I could find. I had my daughter by then and, well I wasn't winning any father-of-the-year awards anyway, but going to jail wasn't going to help, ya know?"

He stood and walked a few paces away, took another hit from his vape pen, blew the steam away from them, and sat back down.

Very considerate, Austin thought.

"But these feds, they had bigger plans," he continued. "They wanted me to go undercover, *deep* undercover. The idea was for me to buddy up with the top dogs, get embedded, then help take down the whole operation from the inside. Problem was, I never *met* any top dogs."

"Just a couple mutts?" Sy asked.

"Exactly. Dude named Manny approached me when he heard I was amenable to certain arrangements and from there it was simple. Three years I brought drugs in from the east in number ten cans. You know, the big ones full of tomatoes, or beans or whatever. *Ten Can Man,* they called me. Never even saw a grain of the powder myself. When we'd dock anywhere in southeast Asia, I was in charge of overseeing the food re-stocking. And there were always about thirty cans of baked beans or corn or whatever marked with a little Shamrock on the bottom. That told me not to cook 'em. I ran the kitchen, so it was no biggie. When we came back home, three months, six months later, dude would come get them."

"What dude?" Sy asked. "Manny?"

"Nah. White guy, but not Italian, not Jewish. He was Navy, or at least he had a uniform. Looked like, I don't know, surfer type dude. But that's the thing. I know he worked for The Nightmare, too, but we never talked about it. My job was just to not use those cans and make sure I was there for the offload. Like I said, I was small time. So was Manny. Always got the sense that there were a hundred Mannys out there, a hundred Joey Greens. And not just in the Navy. They smuggled product a hundred different ways."

"You said a little shamrock on the cans?" Austin asked.

"Yeah, a little stamp right next to the expiration date. You had to know where to look."

"And Manny?" Sy asked. "Where did he end up?"

"He died a year into it, got hit by a drunk driver, or so I heard. I got a letter saying nothing would change, so I kept looking for those cans and giving 'em to the surfer-type dude."

"And how'd they pay you?" Austin asked.

"Oh yeah, forgot about that. One of the cans was always marked with a shamrock along with this little flower thing, I don't know. Hard to explain. Funny, that can was always a little heavier than the rest. Twenty grand cash. Always the same. It wasn't heavier on account of the cash, though. They filled the bottom of it with concrete, so you wouldn't know it wasn't filled with food. But, yeah, those ones were heavier." He chuckled. "Feds even let me keep half of the money so it wouldn't look like I was too broke, those bastards. Anyway, finally I got busted. Someone snitched. Local cops brought me in and I figured, I'm good. The feds aren't jokers, I thought, they're gonna step up and set things right. But the feds didn't let the local boys in on it, and those prosecutors thought they'd caught a real celebrity drug lord." He smiled. "Little old Joey Green from Jersey."

"So what happened?" Sy asked.

"Radio silence. Left me on read, as the kids say. I was the Devil with an empty net, no goalie in sight. Dishonorably discharged and the feds cut me loose to keep my cover, didn't care that I was doing time."

"But you only ended up doing a couple years of a ten year sentence," Sy said. "Maybe the feds intervened on your behalf?"

"That's the weird part," Joey said. "I have no idea *how* my sentence got commuted."

"The governor signed the order," Austin said.

"Well, yeah, but he's a businessman," Joey said. "Who's pulling the strings? Might have been the feds righting an old wrong. Might have been The Nightmare, figuring I'd proved I wasn't a snitch."

Austin considered this. Sure, it was possible that the governor had been doing someone a favor, but it was also possible the favor was for himself. After all, he was one of the five people on Fiona's list.

"So," Sy said, "you mentioned The Nightmare..."

"He was the boss, at least that's what Manny told me. And I think the surfer bro mentioned him once, too."

"You sure it was a him?" Sy asked.

Joey considered this, then shook his head. "Guess I'm kinda sexist. Coulda been a lady."

"Ever heard of another nickname for this person?" Austin asked.

Joey scrunched up his face. "Feds asked me that once, when I was giving them a report. I never heard no other name for the boss, but they said that whoever was running this thing had two names. One was The Nightmare. The other was The Magician."

Austin listened to the wind rustle the trees above him. It was an interesting piece of information, but the truth was, having another nickname for the mastermind didn't bring them much closer to figuring out who it was.

He stood and walked in a little circle. The pain in his shoulder was growing so intense he had to move around to keep it at bay. "Did you ever get the sense that the thing went higher up in the Navy?"

"That I can say for sure, it didn't. We may have worked for a pro, but our stuff was amateur hour, man. No one in the Navy knew except for a couple low level scrubs like me." He shook his head. "Nah, whoever was behind this was outside."

"I'm gonna come right out with it," Austin said. "Mayor McKinley. Lieutenant Governor Mark Richardson. FBI Director Walter Perkins. Any of those three have a connection that you know about?"

Joey said nothing.

"Could any of those three be The Nightmare, The Magician?"

"New York is corrupt as hell. *Any* one of those three could be, but I have no idea which one, or if it's someone else entirely."

CHAPTER TWENTY-NINE

THE STENCH of fish was getting to him.

The coarse rope chafed Jorge's wrists as he slowly twisted and maneuvered his hands.

It had taken him an hour to regain consciousness after the beating. He was bruised and battered and bloodied, but he wasn't *dead*. And he hadn't told them a damn thing.

For now, that was enough.

His training had taught him how to methodically work bindings, even through excruciating pain. So he twisted and pulled, incrementally loosening the constricting ropes. The fibers were tight, expertly woven through layers of intricate knots by his captors.

Jorge focused on finding any weakness in the ropework, some minuscule slack or lapse in tension. He kept his movements subtle, imperceptible just in case they were watching him.

A storm seemed to be passing overhead as Jorge worked. With each tiny shift of his hands, he could feel the knots giving way ever so slightly. A millimeter here, a millimeter there. Escape would be a slow, grinding process, and that was assuming they didn't kill him first.

Jorge's mind wandered to the night he first met Maria—over twenty years ago. He'd just started with the FBI and was still getting accustomed to the city. That chilly autumn evening, he had ducked into a cozy jazz club after a long day at the office. A sultry singer took the stage, and Jorge was instantly captivated by both her voice and beauty. They struck up a conversation between sets and, later, they strolled the city streets till sunrise. Maria moved with such grace, eyes sparkling as she shared dreams of singing on bigger stages. When morning's light peeked through the skyscrapers, Jorge knew he'd found someone special. She became his wife soon after, and the memory of their magical first night stayed vivid through all the years. She'd never landed on the biggest stages, but she still sang twice a week at the same jazz club. What he wouldn't give to be sitting in that audience again, listening to her voice.

Focusing on his task, he tuned out the thunder and ignored the rain dripping through cracks in the roof of the old warehouse. He had one objective: keep loosening, keep progressing, no matter how long it took, no matter how little progress he made.

Assuming they were going to shoot him, eventually police would find his body. When they did, he wanted them to find that he'd worked the bindings at least slightly loose.

He wanted them to be able to tell Maria that he'd used his last hours trying to escape. That he hadn't given up. That he'd tried his best to make it home to her.

CHAPTER THIRTY

"I THINK I was wrong to come out here," Austin said as Joey disappeared back onto the ferry. "I was definitely wrong to involve *you*. I'm sorry."

Sy turned toward him. "I'm not. As crazy as it sounds, I'm enjoying myself."

A light rain began to fall, ending the run of clear weather they'd had.

Austin stretched his legs out in front of him and he leaned back, the rain chilling his skin and the depth of his pain and exhaustion hitting him all at once. "We're nowhere. That's the truth."

"What do you mean? You have Fiona's list of suspects, you've eliminated two of them and—"

Austin stood suddenly. "We have three suspects, and that's assuming Fiona was even right. It could also be someone else. And we have no real way to find anything on them. Not to mention, they're three of the most powerful people in the state, the country. I don't know what the hell I was thinking."

Austin began strolling in the direction of the ferry, which was boarding for the return trip back to New York City. Sy stood and jogged a few paces to catch up with him.

"I've never heard you sound so down," Sy said. "It's not like you, this self-pity."

The phrase struck him hard, but not hard enough to pull him out of it. He shoved his hands in his pockets and stared up at the Statue of Liberty. At any other time, he might have marveled at its size, its stoic beauty. He might have reflected on what it represented, been inspired to read a book about its creation and how and why the French had built it and gifted it to America.

But, to his shame, as they boarded the ferry he found himself searching for a thought, a phrase to try to justify his self-pity. Then his phone rang. It was a 360 number, the area code for much of Kitsap County back home. He'd only given this number to two people: Kendall and the vet.

"Hello?"

"Is this Thomas Austin?"

"Yes, this is Austin. Is this about Run?"

"The corgi, yes, and I'm sorry but we don't have great news, Mr. Austin."

Austin's stomach turned to stone. It was as though his body was anticipating the worst and he tasted ice. But not a normal cold, neutral ice. It was like ice left uncovered in the freezer for years, growing freezer burned to the point that it could ruin any drink into which it was placed.

"We thought we were in the clear after the surgery, but unfortunately Run has taken a turn for the worse," the vet said. "Her amylase and lipase levels have spiked back up, indicating her pancreatitis is flaring again. This has also caused some other complications. She's developed pneumonia, and her kidney values are showing signs of acute kidney injury. Basically her pancreas is inflamed and the vomiting led to aspirating food or fluids causing the pneumonia. Her kidneys are stressed from the dehydration."

Austin's mouth was cold, dry, but he heard words coming out from it. "What does that mean right now? Does she need another surgery? Will she recover?"

"We won't need further surgery. But she'll likely need to stay a few more days for IV fluids, antibiotics, and medications to manage the pancreatitis flare. We'll give supportive care with fluids and monitor her closely. Most dogs recover well with this more conservative treatment once the initial inflammation is reduced surgically. I'm optimistic given her initial improvement, but wanted you to be aware that it may be a longer recovery than we initially anticipated. Hope for the best, prepare for the worst. We'll be giving her the best care possible."

The next words out of his mouth came before he'd even registered them as a thought. "I'm in New York, but I'll be flying back tonight. I'll get there as soon as I can."

CHAPTER THIRTY-ONE

AUSTIN'S HEAD thumped against the window and, for half a second, he was awake. Opening his eyes briefly. He saw New York City disappearing behind him. "How much further?"

The taxi driver spoke in a thick Russian accent. "JFK ten minutes."

He took one more look at Manhattan, hazy and rainy and gray and bleak. Good riddance, he thought.

He'd stopped by the hotel to pick up a few things, said an awkward goodbye to Sy during which he'd probably apologized too many times for involving her in this, then hopped in the first taxi he could find. He'd been asleep within minutes, the pain in his shoulder somehow combining with his splitting headache to knock him right out.

Now, ten minutes from the airport, all he wanted to do was sleep. And as he drifted back into it, this time he dreamed.

~

He was walking down the beach in Hansville, worried because Run wasn't there. As he walked he grew more and more concerned. Why was the sand white and red? Where was Run? Her toys were there. Her little yellow frisbee, three or four tennis balls in various states of destruction, even a rubber chew toy he thought had been lost.

But where was Run?

He began hurrying down the beach. But the sand was wet and turning all to red and he kept sinking in and he lost his shoes, but he kept running and running and running and looking and looking.

Then he was on his hands and knees looking for Run under logs and inside bushes and behind rocks. But she was nowhere. He was sinking into wet, red sand and couldn't breathe.

Suddenly he was somewhere else. An Upper West Side dog shelter with Fiona and they were talking about having a baby and she kept suggesting ridiculous baby names like Pinesol and Cabinet and Ice Cream.

And she was eating ice cream, too. Mint chip, her favorite.

But why were they at a dog shelter and why did the conversation keep oscillating back and forth between getting a dog and having a baby? They couldn't decide, and all the dogs started barking at once, louder and louder, hitting every tone, every note, until Austin couldn't hear Fiona anymore. And she kept smiling and eating her ice cream and listing off baby names even though Austin could no longer hear her.

Then he was at work and he was a young man and still looking for Run around his old NYPD office. His shoes were gone, his feet covered in red sand.

He looked for Run under a table in the break room. Behind the reception desk. In the evidence room.

And then he was looking for Fiona, and then Run again, and then Fiona again and he still had no shoes on. He looked in old filing cabinets and in desk drawers and behind the water cooler and kept looking and looking. He was repeatedly bumping his shoulder into doors and walls, so it hurt more and more the longer he looked. And all the while he grew younger until he was just a boy, maybe ten years old, wandering around an NYPD evidence room all by himself, late at night, getting lost amidst the tall shelves piled with boxes.

And his friend David was there. His friend who had died. His troubled and brilliant friend from the NYPD.

And David began quoting books and films, trying to tell Austin what to do. Something about how he needed to find out what his cathedral was and build it. But the dogs were barking again, and Fiona was trying to tell him baby names and he couldn't hear Fiona or David or anyone. Just the barking dogs.

He studied the strange look on David's face as though he might be able to read his lips. He started to make out words.

The

It

Poetry

Elevator

Deadly

Similar

All the individual words made sense, but didn't make sense together, didn't form a coherent sentence, and then Austin realized that David didn't have the answer. David didn't even know the question. David was just mouthing random words. He was messing with him.

And then David's face turned into Austin's father's face and he kept speaking and Austin kept studying his lips.

Death

Western

Mother

Afraid

He saw the words forming on his father's lips, but still he couldn't make out any meaning out of them.

Silence

Death

Graphic
Death
Death
Death

Austin's head bumped against the window and he woke up.

Immediately he closed his eyes tight, trying to keep the dream going, trying to put the words together into something coherent, into something with meaning.

What were David and his father trying to tell him?

"Almost there," the taxi driver said, oblivious to the disturbing worlds Austin had just been pulled through.

He reached for his wallet, shook his head back and forth and pressed his palms into his cheeks. He took out sixty bucks and grabbed his duffel bag from the seat next to him, placing it on his lap.

Austin didn't dream much, or at least he rarely remembered his dreams. Standing in the ticket line, he was still in a daze.

He'd read a few chapters of a pop psychology book about dreams once, most of which sounded like gibberish to him. But one piece of advice had stuck with him despite his cynicism: *When thinking about your dreams, don't focus only on what happened, focus instead on how it felt. What was the emotional state you were in while watching the story of the dream unfold?*

Some of the dream made sense, the meanings were obvious. Looking for Run, looking for Fiona. Jumping between his new home and his old home. He didn't remember ever going to a dog shelter with Fiona. In the dream that had been like a memory, but he didn't think it had ever happened. He would remember that. They had talked about getting a dog and talked about having kids, but they'd never done either. But mint chip was indeed her favorite. And she had once suggested a string of ridiculous baby names.

He thought about how David had morphed into his father. Though he had never thought of David as a father figure, he felt like he had let David down in the same way that he'd let his father down. His father, whose dementia was getting worse and worse, and who he didn't call as much as he should.

He didn't think all the words David and his father had mouthed actually meant anything. He tried focusing on how he'd felt during that part of the dream, not the meaning. All he'd felt was confusion, like a kid called on in class, a kid who didn't know the answer and didn't have his hand raised in the first place. All he wanted was to know the answer.

To know the answer.

It struck him that that was all he ever wanted. That there was a kind of burning inside him. When his synesthesia kicked in it sometimes came with the ping of a tart cherry flavor that turned his mind to fire. That was what drove him.

Sometimes he thought of himself as not having any moral code. He'd lost touch with his religion at a young age and he knew as well as anyone that some laws were just and others unjust. And that some law enforcement officers were just and others not so much. It was as though he'd lost all his bearings, had nothing to cling to except his desire to know the answer.

Then it struck him: none of that mattered.

If finding the answer was what excited him, *that* was enough, and he had to keep looking.

Standing outside, waiting for a taxi, he called Kendall. Her phone went straight to voicemail.

"It is me, Austin." He moved a few paces forward in the line. "I won't be back for at least another couple days. Or maybe not at all. I spoke with the vet and they said Run took a turn. They probably called you as well. I almost decided to come back, but I need to see this out."

He was next in line and a taxi pulled up. "Financial district," he said as he got in. Then, back on the phone, he continued, "I don't know for sure if I'll be coming back. I should probably just admit that. If I don't, please do three things for me. Go get Run and let her live with you and Ralph. And if you want you can have my apartment. Give my store and café to Andy. He's been my number two there for a while and has been doing most of the work anyways. He's good at it. Tell him that for me. And, Fiona's red peacoat—it was her favorite. Please make sure it gets to her niece Olive. I just hope it's what's in style by the time it fits her, although I think it's the sort of look that's timeless. You guys can work out the details. But if I don't come back, consider this my last will and testament."

CHAPTER THIRTY-TWO

THE CASHIER OFFERED a fake smile in Sy's general direction, then looked at her a little closer and, when he finally got his eyes off her chest, offered up a real one. "What can I get you? Other than my number."

Sy studied the menu, written in colorful chalk on a giant board behind the espresso machine. She gave the cashier a wry smile. "First of all, what are you, twenty? I'm way too old for you. And I'll take a half double decaf oat milk latte with a lime wedge and salted rim."

The young man looked confused and looked shakily at the menu board. "I, umm, I don't know if we have that."

"Bad joke, sorry. Triple cappuccino."

He hit himself in the forehead with an open palm. "Oh, right. I was serious about giving you my number, though. And I'm twenty-two. What are you, twenty-nine?"

Sy gave him her best *no-chance-in-hell-kid* look. "I'm forty." Actually, she was a little flattered. He was roughly half her age, but a good looking young man and it had never bothered her when men were forward, as long as they took "No" for an answer when she delivered it.

He frowned. "Okay," he said after struggling for a long time to find the right things to tap on his order screen. "Name for the order?"

"Symone."

"It'll be a minute. We're cleaning out the machine."

"No worries." She paid and glanced around the lobby of the hotel. She'd gotten her stuff and figured she'd check out while waiting for the coffee.

She'd tried the same *half double decaf oat milk latte* joke on Austin when they'd met in his little café. He'd at least courtesy chuckled. He was a good guy that way. Even when confronted with a terrible joke like that, he'd offer up a little laugh. It wasn't that he was faking it. He knew as well as anyone that it wasn't funny and he wasn't pretending otherwise. It was like he wanted to maintain a connection with her. And giving her a chuckle was more of an acknowledgment than an attempt to convince her that the joke was any good.

He was much more her type than a twenty-something cashier, actually. At least, she'd thought so. Maybe he had a concussion, maybe he was worried about his dog, or maybe something else was going on. But she'd been surprised and disappointed that he'd decided to bail.

She glanced at the barista and cashier, who finally seemed to have the espresso machine working again, then let her gaze fall on the large windows that looked out onto the street. A silver van had double parked out front. There was nothing unusual about that in New York City, except that an older man seemed to be leaning up against it, gasping for air.

He was holding himself up, and looked almost like he was having a heart attack.

Sy hurried out and approached the man. "Sir, are you okay?"

He coughed and gasped for air. Sy reached for his shoulder to try to turn him toward her. "I'll call 911. Sir, just try to breathe."

The back door of the van swung open and, at the same

moment, she felt large, meaty hands on her shoulders from behind.

Following her training, she kicked up hard with her heel, striking the man who'd grabbed her in the groin. She tried to turn, but the man who'd been choking and gasping for air was suddenly fine.

He grabbed her in a headlock, rammed her head against the door of the van.

Her eyes went blurry and, before she knew what was happening, she'd been shoved into the back of the van. Someone was grabbing at her, rummaging through her pockets. She could barely see through her watering eyes. She punched and clawed, but he'd already grabbed her phone. The door slammed and locked behind her.

Moments later the van was moving.

A metal divider split the back of the van from the front.

She was in a cage.

CHAPTER THIRTY-THREE

AUSTIN CALLED Sy for the second time from the taxi, but she wasn't answering. When he'd left for the airport, she'd told him she was going to hang out at the hotel for a bit, then check out and head back to Connecticut. He shot her a text. In case she had her ringer off, she might see her screen light up with his message. Maybe she was still upset with him. And she had every right to be. He'd dragged her into this, then bailed at the eleventh hour.

Plus, she had a life to piece back together. From what she'd told him, her records search for Joey Green would be forgiven. After all, she hadn't knowingly tried to access information she wasn't allowed. If anything, she had a right to be upset that somehow his file had been classified in a way that didn't follow standard procedure.

Austin paid for the taxi and headed back into the lobby of the hotel. He stopped at the elevator, then turned toward the check in desk. He decided he should confirm that she'd checked out. After all, she expected him to be on a flight back to Washington by now. It would likely come as quite a surprise if he appeared at the hotel room door unannounced.

"Hello," he said when the man behind the counter asked how he could help him. "I'm Mr. Jackson. My wife Mrs. Jackson, did she check out already?"

The man tapped on his screen. "No, sir. We have you down for one more night."

"Could you call up to the room?" She's not answering her phone.

Austin watched as the man called, waited, hung up. "She's not answering your guest room phone, Mr. Jackson."

Austin considered this. Possibly she'd decided to do something else around the city. "Could you try once more?"

The man did. "No answer at her extension, sir."

"Maybe she's still out and about," Austin said, but he wasn't convinced. Something was wrong.

The man said, "I do believe I saw Mrs. Jackson in the lobby, maybe an hour ago."

"And did you see where she went?"

He shook his head. "I'm sorry, sir."

"Thanks anyway," Austin said, but his worry was only intensifying.

Sitting at one of the little tables in the lobby café, he stretched out his long legs and thought. Perhaps Sy had gone to look for more information on the case herself. But, if so, why wouldn't she be answering her phone?

"Closing in five minutes!" A young man behind the cash register called out.

Austin ambled up to the counter. "Black coffee, please."

The kid got the coffee and Austin paid, returning to his seat.

Or perhaps she'd decided to head straight back to Connecticut. After all, she didn't have much up in the room. Perhaps she'd decided to wipe her hands of the whole thing. And good for her if she had.

"Symone!"

Austin's head shot up in the direction of the shout. It was the barista, holding a white paper coffee cup and looking confused. "Symone, your triple cappuccino."

Austin hurried up to the counter, where the cashier was explaining something to the barista. "Bro, I think she left, man. That was like an hour ago."

"The woman who ordered it," Austin said, hurriedly. "Was she kinda tall, black hair?"

The young man's face reddened. "Hot, too. I was gonna give her my best line when she came back for her drink, but she never came back."

"Did you see where she went?"

He shook his head. "Maybe, like, outside, or…"

If Sy had ordered a coffee but not picked it up, there was a chance she'd forgotten it. But that chance was so small he didn't even really consider it.

Something had happened to her.

Austin hurried back to the front desk. "Where's the security office?"

"It's, um, in the basement, next to the fitness room, but—"

Austin was already heading for the stairs. Bounding down them two at a time, he nearly toppled over. When he reached the bottom of the stairs, he looked both ways, then followed the signs toward the gym and banged on the unmarked brown door next to it.

The door opened slowly, revealing a tiny security office—more of a closet, really—and a man who looked as bored as anyone Austin had ever seen. He seemed out of place in his ill-fitting navy blue security uniform, probably a size too large for his slender frame. Tufts of wiry gray hair peeked out from under his cap and his weathered face was angled down, eyes scanning the pages of a magazine splayed open on the desk.

"I need to see your security footage," Austin said.

The guard sat, reclining in a rolling office chair that creaked slightly with each movement. The dull glow of the video monitors lined up on the desk provided most of the dim lighting in the tight space. "I... I can't do that, sir. I'm sorry are you—"

"A woman was abducted—possibly from within your lobby— in the last sixty to ninety minutes. I'm a private investigator and I need to see your footage. Now. Trust me when I tell you that you don't want to have this conversation with the NYPD after I tell them you were reading a magazine instead of monitoring the video."

The man cleared his throat and sat up, sliding his chair back and hovering over a styrofoam coffee cup. "It'll take me a minute, a few minutes. Ninety minutes back, you say? Lobby footage?"

Austin nodded. "I'll be right back."

Stepping into the hallway outside the fitness room, out of earshot of the security guard, he dialed Samantha. When she picked up, Austin said. "Is there any way to track someone's location through their cell phone?"

"Nice to hear from you, too, Austin."

"I don't have time for banter."

"Buddy, this is *me* you're talking to. Of course there's a way," Samantha said, "but it depends on a lot. Tell me what's going on."

"Sy, my friend. I think she may have been taken." He paused, taking in a deep breath of stale, fitness center air as someone walked out.

"If she was taken, it's unlikely her phone is still on."

Austin cursed under his breath. "Of course, but can you check anyway?"

"On the record, no. It's illegal as hell, and will take a minute, but yeah, my boyfriend can see if her phone pinged any towers recently."

Austin gave her Sy's number, then hurried back into the cramped security office.

CHAPTER THIRTY-FOUR

THE PROCESS of looking through the security footage was agonizingly slow and inefficient.

For a moment, Austin wished he was on one of those television crime shows where an attractive twenty-something tech expert tapped keys at lightning speed and zoomed in frame by frame to get a clear headshot of the villain without losing any resolution.

Sitting in a cramped, smelly, office with a rude, uninterested security guard was a lot less dramatic.

And it gave him time to consider something: how had they found Sy at the hotel? And as soon as he asked himself the question, he landed on an answer: Mara Graves. Although it was possible they'd tracked them some other way, the easiest explanation was that Mara had sold them out.

He'd been a fool to trust her, but he didn't have time to beat himself up about it.

"Well," the guard finally said with a sigh, "this is the time period, but I don't see anything that would help."

The monitor showed a wide shot of the lobby taken from behind the front desk. Apparently, this was the camera designed to track who came in and who came out, and it clearly showed Sy coming in through the main entrance, then walking to the café to order a coffee. Although it wasn't a close-up, Austin could see her long, straight black hair, and she even glanced up toward the camera for a minute as though she knew it was there.

Then it showed her walking toward the front entrance of the hotel, but she disappeared after that as the footage lost track of her.

"What other cameras do you have?" Austin asked.

"We have one in the coffee shop, which we added after a robbery a few years ago." He turned halfway in his chair to face Austin. His breath smelled like wine and coffee, and Austin tried to ignore the fact that he may have been drinking on the job. "Homeless guy on drugs bust through the door, stole a couple hundred bucks in cash. He didn't even have a gun. He threatened the barista with a broken bottle."

Austin gently turned him back to the screen. "Can you pull that one up? The coffee shop."

Austin wished Samantha was here when he saw how slowly the security guard clicked through the little frames on his computer. But eventually, he found another clip and, over the course of a few minutes, found the right time period.

"There!" Austin said, way too loud for the cramped space. "That's it."

The video showed Sy hurrying out the glass door and walking up to a man who was leaning on the side of a van.

"Oh, no!" he whispered. He'd seen this type of thing before. He'd worked multiple cases of robberies and kidnappings in which perpetrators worked in tandem, one pretending to be hurt or injured, the other stepping in to commit the crime when the victim was distracted by their own attempt to help.

He was surprised it had worked on Sy, but she was a helpful person, a giving person. Perhaps she'd relaxed, thinking their investigation was over.

On the screen, it played out exactly as he'd feared. The man who was pretending to be ill was in his sixties, with a vaguely European look. He had a slight build and wore a dark hat and thick glasses.

"Oh no," the guard said when the doors of the van opened.

Austin stopped breathing.

The man who leapt out and abducted Sy was harder to identify because he only showed his back to the camera. In seconds, she'd been shoved into the back of the van.

But at least she was alive.

"Pause it!" Austin said suddenly. "Go back, rewind." The van had made a quick u-turn across two lanes of traffic, exposing its license plate briefly. "Go back a couple seconds."

The security guard went back too far, then fast-forwarded too far, then went back too far again, forcing Austin to watch Sy's abduction again.

But finally, they landed in the right place.

A clear shot of the van's license plate number.

Austin jotted it down on a spare piece of paper from the man's cluttered desk, then said, "Call the police. Tell them what happened. Give them the plate number. Give them the footage. Do anything you can."

To his shock, the man seemed either confused or, worse, uninterested. Austin stood, grabbed him by the collar of his shirt, and got right in his face. "This woman was just abducted on your watch. This is already bad, but it could get way worse for you. Or, you could be the hero. The one who was *definitely* watching the footage like his job description says and called the police the moment he noticed something was up. Have a cup of coffee, chew a stick of minty gum, and get the police out here immediately. "

CHAPTER THIRTY-FIVE

SAMANTHA SAT BACK and stared at the financial transactions on her screen, eyes wide. "That's not possible," she said to herself.

She didn't think of herself as a paranoid person, but she glanced around the little makeshift office in Ridley's campaign headquarters, worried that someone was watching her.

She was all alone, as she had been for hours.

She'd been working to trace the donations and wire transfers of tech billionaire Talus Aaron Ockley and what she'd stumbled upon left her in shock. She'd always assumed that politics was fairly corrupt, but what she was staring at was a level she'd never even considered.

Finding the information had been challenging. She'd started by scouring public databases and financial records for abnormal transactions linked to Ockley. Next, with the help of her boyfriend, she'd developed algorithms to identify patterns in Ockley's financial behavior that human eyes would miss. Together they'd used their knowledge of network security to access dozens of encrypted databases, then painstakingly cross-referenced the data with the names of politicians, their relatives, and known associates. It had been a laborious process, but their expertise in data mining, network security, and digital forensics had eventually unearthed Ockley's web of corruption.

Over the course of the last twelve months, Ockley had funneled hundreds of millions of dollars to politicians on both sides of the aisle. He was a well-known political contributor, there was nothing new about that. But in addition to all of his *legal* contributions, he'd made dozens of wire transfers to offshore companies owned by third-parties linked to politicians in dozens of countries.

The range of Ockley's illegal contributions astounded her. There were five main kinds of fraud, each more stunning than the last.

First, he was donating to offshore shell companies under the names of politicians' relatives or other confidants. This obscured the money trail back to him.

Second, he would hire politicians as "consultants" for his companies, paying them huge fees for little work as a cover for bribes.

Next was his manipulation of real estate, snapping up properties owned by politicians at inflated prices to funnel wealth. Then there were donations to fraudulent charities controlled by the politicians, mere fronts for his dealings.

And finally, he used cryptocurrencies to transfer funds to politicians' digital wallets, making the source untraceable when converted back to cash.

She glanced up at the wall, where the countdown clock to the close of voting had hit fourteen hours. Uncovering Ockley's web of deceit left her filled with dread. Partially because it was her job to find the juiciest morsels related to Sheriff Grayson Daniels and use it to sink his campaign right up until the buzzer. And partially because Ockley's donations connected to some of the people Austin had asked her to research as well. She didn't precisely know *why*, but she liked Austin. He was a bit of a cliché, of course, but still. He was a good guy. And she hated the fact that his investigation touched on Ockley, a man more powerful than most countries.

In the latest internal polling, Carter had dropped down even further, but a series of high-profile paid advertisements had Daniels on the rise. Ridley had received a slight bump, too, likely caused by his last couple days of campaigning, which had taken him on a whirlwind trip through most of the counties in Washington State.

He'd kissed babies, tasted local apple cider, visited college campuses, ridden a fishing boat, attended a ceremony hosted by one of the local tribes, even knocked on doors to introduce himself to voters in Seattle and Tacoma.

As far as Samantha could tell, he'd done everything he could. He was still slightly behind, but with enough undecided voters left to give him a shot.

Grayson Daniels: 35%
Ridley Calvin: 33%
Jeremy Carter: 26%
Undecided: 6%

Her phone rang and she recognized Austin's new number. "Hey," she said, "I've got bad news. Sy's phone was either turned off or destroyed."

It had taken her boyfriend an hour to get into the system that kept track of cell phone locations, but only a few seconds to determine that Sy's phone had not pinged any cellphone towers in quite some time. Not a surprise, assuming Austin was right that she'd been abducted.

She heard Austin let out a long stream of air, but what he said next surprised her.

"How fast can you get me info from a license plate number?"

"Minutes," Samantha said, opening a new window on her laptop. "You got the car that took her?"

"One of the upsides to the fact that there are surveillance cameras everywhere these days."

Austin read her the number.

"Gimme three minutes," she said. "Assuming I get an address, I'll message you through Signal."

"Great, thanks."

"And Austin, there's something else. On those people you asked me to look into, I—"

"I don't have time for that now," Austin interrupted. "Just get me any info on that van."

CHAPTER THIRTY-SIX

AUSTIN REFRESHED his Signal app for the fifth time. Still nothing from Samantha.

Leaning on a parking meter around the corner from the hotel, horns blared around him and a cold rain began to fall. Traffic seemed to be stopped in all directions. And he was watching like a hawk. He'd grabbed the taser from the room and holstered it on his left hip after reorienting himself to its mechanism of action. Between that and his gun, he felt... well, not safe, but as safe as he was going to get.

He'd already hurried back down to the basement to make sure the security guard had contacted the NYPD. He had, and they were on their way. He'd decided not to be there when they arrived. Chances were, they would be none too keen on his involvement in the case, but with the video footage they'd likely take action. At the same time, he didn't trust them to treat the abduction with the same urgency he would.

He'd be pursuing this on his own.

Finally, his phone vibrated with a message from Samantha.

Van is registered to:

Rosalyn Abramowitz, Apartment 5C

112 Orchard Apple Avenue
New York, NY 10003
No criminal record. Lifelong resident of Manhattan's Lower East Side neighborhood with a history of work as a waitress and performer at local bars. She has lived at that address for over 40 years.

Austin tapped the address into the maps app on his phone. It was only 1.8 miles away, and, with the traffic the way it was, he figured he'd be better off jogging.

Twenty minutes later, soaking wet from rain and sweat, Austin banged on the door of apartment 5C. The building was a rare 5-story walkup, the sort of building that had been everywhere in the seventies and eighties but had mostly been renovated or torn down entirely.

A gray-haired woman opened the door, wearing a robe over her pants and sweater.

"Rosalyn Abramowitz?" Austin asked.

"Michael, is that you?" She squinted at him, shaking her head in what seemed to be a nervous tic of some sort. Maybe a side effect from some sort of long term use medication she'd been taking.

"No, my name is Thomas Austin. I'm looking for a missing woman who was taken in a van registered in your name. May I come in?"

The woman looked confused. "A van?" The smell from the apartment—combined with her raspy voice—told Austin she'd likely been on the two-packs-a-day plan for many, many years.

"Yes, registered to you. Ma'am, this is very serious."

"Fine, fine," she said. "Would you like a cup of tea, young man?"

Ten minutes later, Rosalyn stood in her cramped kitchen, peering out between two curtains into the alley below, waiting for her tea kettle to heat up. Austin thought the curtains must have once been a pristine white. Now a dull ivory, they were covered with black specks that were either mold or bits of food that were about to mold.

Austin had tried five different ways of asking her about the van and she either knew nothing about it or she was the best liar he'd ever encountered. As out of touch as she seemed, it was quite possible that someone had used her name and address on the registration. And if that was the case, he needed to find out if it was someone she knew.

The problem was, she was confused and not especially forthcoming.

"Who are they?" Austin asked, pointing at a row of five small photos on the kitchen wall.

This seemed to get her attention.

Leaning on her medical grade cane, Rosalyn sighed, the sound crackling through lungs worn by a lifetime of breathing in city air through cigarette filters. Then she smoothed her olive cardigan gently, a trace of her youthful poise still evident in the simple gesture, and pointed up at the photos.

Each had been framed in a thin gold frame and each needed a good cleaning. Years of cooking grease and dust had left a thin film over each, but Austin could still make out the faces of the people he assumed were her relatives.

"My grandchildren." She wandered over slowly, then pointed at the one on the far left. "That's little Joey there, he's eight and obsessed with rocks." She moved from left to right as she continued. "And here's Katie in the soccer uniform, she's twelve and kicks that ball harder than any boy on the team. My Jamie just turned fifteen, he's, well, I don't know what he does but he sure is handsome. Like my husband."

"And where is your husband?"

She frowned. "In a box in the Bronx. Cedarwood Cemetery."

Austin cleared his throat. "I'm sorry."

"And this," she continued, "is Michael here with the frown. He's eighteen and into some trouble these days. And last is my Sarah, she's twenty and off studying art history at some fancy college upstate." She leaned in and whispered conspiratorially. "She's dating another woman, which I used to be against until I met her last boyfriend, Chaz. What a loser!"

"Tell me more about Michael," Austin said.

She shook her head. "He's a good boy deep down."

Austin saw her thinking and chose his next words carefully. "And you have *no idea* why a van might be registered in your name?"

"You're with the police, right?"

"Not exactly," Austin admitted.

"So you probably can't help me with these, then?" She waved a few envelopes at him, then held them close to her chest. "Parking tickets," she said. "Like I told you, I don't even own a car, and I haven't been to Brooklyn in years."

Austin tried to contain his emotion, which was somewhere between excitement and anger. If she'd gotten a series of parking tickets she didn't understand, how could she not have put that together with his questions about the van?

"May I see those?" Austin asked.

She handed them to him and turned back to her tea kettle. "C'mon, c'mon," she coaxed.

Austin spread them out on the table. There were five altogether and he arranged them so their addresses were all visible.

All of the tickets had been issued in Brooklyn and, though he didn't recognize all of the street names, he recognized two of them. They weren't far from the hotel where he'd been staying in Manhattan Beach.

Next he yanked out his phone and took a series of pictures, making sure to get each address clearly. Seconds later, while

Rosalyn was still speaking with her tea kettle, the photo of the tickets was en route to Samantha with the following note.

Urgent: Please look at these five addresses and tell me something: where is the most likely place this person was going when he got these five tickets? That is, assuming the same person got these five parking tickets and each time they were going to the same place, where would that place be?

Next, Austin leapt up and snapped a photo of the picture of Michael in the gold frame.

The tea kettle whistled and Rosalyn turned around, holding it with a pot holder. "You know," she said. "He told me no one would ever come asking about it, that everything was okay." She sighed and poured the water in the sink. It appeared as though she'd forgotten about the tea. "He's a good boy deep down."

CHAPTER THIRTY-SEVEN

"YOU'RE AN UTTER PIECE OF CRAP," Sy said to the man who'd faked being ill to lure her toward the van. "And I wonder, have you always been like that, or is it a recent development?"

"Shut up!" the man barked.

"I mean, you couldn't have been born this way, right? And you definitely weren't born smelling this way."

The man said nothing.

With the help of the larger, younger man, she'd been tied to a chair in what smelled like a fish store or warehouse. They'd blindfolded her in the van so she couldn't be sure, but she thought another captive was nearby. She could hear someone breathing heavily and groaning softly from time to time. She assumed it must be Jorge. But she didn't say anything. She didn't want the men to know she sensed his presence there.

She could place the two men by the way they moved and the sound of their footsteps. In her mind she was calling them Old Guy and Fat Guy. Not especially creative, but she didn't care.

In all likelihood she'd be dead soon, so there was no point in coming up with kinder nicknames. Plus, she didn't plan on checking out without a fight.

She heard Old Guy whispering something to Fat Guy, then a door creaked open and another set of footsteps entered. These were quicker, lighter footsteps. *Light Foot*, she decided.

Then she heard a new voice. "We've almost got this thing wrapped up," the voice said. And she thought she might recognize it. It was a man, not young but not old, she thought, with a kind of odd, ncutral accent. "And Ms. Aoki, we have no interest in you. Truly. We know that, if asked, you'd drop this and return to Connecticut. But Austin..." the speaker paused and Sy could almost hear him shaking his head. "He just won't let this drop. Thinks he can bring his wife's spirit back from the dead or something, I guess."

Three footsteps and she smelled something familiar. Spices mixed with lemon or lime. A cologne, probably.

"Where is he?" the man demanded.

She listened to the heavy silence, opened her mouth, but said nothing. She'd planned to say something snarky, but fear had gripped her.

She knew this person. She was sure of it. She couldn't place him, but she knew him. One thing she was sure of, if this was The Magician, The Nightmare, the one behind it all, she could definitely rule out Mayor McKinley.

After a long silence, the men's footsteps echoed again, the door creaked. This time, Old Guy and Fat Guy followed Light Foot out.

Immediately, she heard the man's voice again, this time shouting at the other two. She could only make out every few words, but it was clear they'd screwed up, and he was not happy about it.

Then, there was silence, and in the silence she heard a scratching sound. "Jorge, is that you?"

"Who are you?" he asked.

"Symone Aoki, NCIS. I was helping Austin. They sent us a video of you. Are you trying to loosen the rope."

"Have been for hours."

"Close?"

"Yeah, another hour, or two maybe. But I'm guessing you don't have a firearm."

"Clear your throat when you've got it," she said. "Just loud enough for me to hear. I've got a plan. I'll cough when it's time for you to bust free."

"I bust free, they're gonna shoot me in the head. What are you gonna do?"

"I'm gonna make him hit me."

The door creaked and the men entered again. Two sets of footsteps. Sy could tell it was only Fat Guy and Old Guy.

Old Guy was already pissed at her, and if they didn't shoot her, she was going to have a little fun with him.

CHAPTER THIRTY-EIGHT

THE RAIN SPATTERED against the taxi's windshield as Austin stepped out, the damp sea air clinging to his skin like a soggy cloak.

Samantha had given him a three-block radius, using the five addresses to identify the most likely location of the driver of the van. He set off at a jog, looking for anything that might trigger his memory, anything that might fit with either of the two hostage videos he'd seen.

He knew he was within a few blocks of the beach where he'd walked only days earlier, only a few blocks, too, from the hotel he'd been staying at. His bet was that Rosalyn's grandson Michael was part of the crew behind this whole thing, probably a low-level, not especially bright member. Most likely he'd registered the van in his grandma's name, thinking that she'd never even notice or that, if she grew suspicious, he could convince her to go along.

A misty haze blurred the edges of the buildings as he jogged past homes, bodegas, and other shops. A salty scent wafted from the Atlantic, mingling with the faint odor of fish and seaweed.

Off to his right, a two-story brick and wood fish market

appeared as he rounded a corner. Paint peeled off the walls in curling flakes. What had once been a vibrant blue was now a weathered, ocean-washed memory. The glass windows were opaque with salt and grime, their filmy glare evidence of years of neglect. The wooden sign out front swayed in the wind, its letters faded almost beyond recognition.

Of all the buildings in the area, it was the most likely spot for a drug front or a gang hangout.

Austin jogged across the deserted street, his boots splashing in the oily puddles. He reached the entrance, unease sinking in as he found the door locked tight. The market was closed, not just for the day, but seemingly for good. He circled the building, his heart throbbing as the rain pelted down on and around him.

The back of the market was all but hidden in a trash-strewn alley, the ground littered with broken crates and discarded nets. He tested the locks on the back door, then the windows, but found them all sealed shut.

He looked up, noticing for the first time an old metal fire escape, rusted from years of salty air and neglect. It ended about eight feet up, out of his reach. With a quick glance at the second floor window a plan formed in his mind. Looking around to confirm he was still alone, he grabbed a stack of wooden crates from further down in the alley.

He dragged two of the sturdiest crates beneath the fire escape's ladder. Climbing onto the makeshift platform, he jumped, his fingers just grazing the bottom rung of the ladder. He crashed hard into the alley, a bolt of pain shooting through his shoulder.

Grimacing, he climbed the crates and leapt again, this time managing to grasp the fire escape firmly.

With a grunt, he hoisted himself up, the metal creaking under his weight. He climbed steadily, the wind and rain threatening his balance. Reaching the second floor, he carefully stepped onto the narrow platform and approached the window.

It was an old sash window, its paint chipped and weather-worn. He took out his wallet and removed an old, laminated card. Sliding it between the sash and the frame, he jiggled it around, applying pressure where the latch might be. With a soft click, the latch gave way, and he carefully raised the window.

He was in.

The room Austin entered was shrouded in darkness, the only light a feebly swaying bulb hanging from a rusted chain. The air was thick with the pungent scent of old fish, salt, and decay, a sickening, musty smell that had seeped into the wooden floors and walls over the years.

Firearm in hand, he moved through the market, his footsteps muffled by the old, damp carpet. He passed a room filled with fishing equipment, his eyes catching on a large fish hook hanging on a peg. The eerie silence was broken by the occasional drip of water from the leaking roof.

Finally, he found a room that appeared to be an office. A room separate from the rest, its door was slightly ajar. He pushed it open, the creak of the hinges echoing in the silence. Instead of carpet, the room had a floor of blue linoleum. The room also had a pine scented air freshener, which combined with the fish stench to create a strange, horrifying smell. There were papers on the desk that were damp. The once high gloss enamel paint on the filing cabinet in the corner was dull and chipped, its top drawer slightly open.

Austin holstered his weapon and began rummaging through the papers in the drawer. Old invoices, delivery notes, receipts. A paper trail of a business that once was. His fingers traced over the faded ink, his heart pounding in his chest as he searched for any clue.

Then, he found it. A delivery note from Brooklyn Seafood Packers. The ink was barely legible, but the address was clear.

It was a warehouse right on the water only a couple blocks

from Manhattan Beach. From the spot where Javier had been killed.

Austin's mind raced.

Reports had said that a little boy had seen two men running down the beach. Javier's body had been found in a pizzeria not far from there.

What if Javier had been held at the warehouse and escaped, and that's why he'd been running down the beach in the first place?

And, more importantly, what if Sy and Jorge were there now?

CHAPTER THIRTY-NINE

JORGE CLEARED HIS THROAT.

The signal.

Sy took a few deep breaths and tilted her head in the direction of Old Man. "Hey, you," she said. "Sounds like you just got reamed." She let that hang in the air for a moment. Since she didn't hear any footsteps, she knew she needed to try again. "Yeah, you old bastard, even your boss seems to know what a screw-up you are." She took another deep breath. There was no going back from this. It had to work. "You are, without a doubt, the most incompetent person who works in the New York City drug trade. What are you, sixty-five? Wait, isn't that retirement age? And this is where life has taken you? Getting berated by a younger boss? Not to mention better-smelling and much handsomer." She paused. "Yeah, I'm blindfolded and I can tell he's better looking than you."

She heard his footsteps. "Shut up, bitch!"

She giggled and, making her voice almost like a little girl, she said, "Oh, that's scary." She put as much mockery into it as she possibly could. "What do you weigh? One-twenty soaking wet? And at least two pounds of that is your stupid, ugly beard. It's a wonder any New Yorkers can still get high if someone like *you* is responsible for the drug trade on the eastern seaboard." She shook her head in feigned disappointment.

The man's footsteps grew closer and closer, and she could smell him. "Say one more word. *One. More. Word.*"

"Oh, I have *plenty* more words..." She felt his slap only a second later. Her cheek burned, but she couldn't have been happier. "That's the best you can do? Bring the big guy over, maybe he has enough weight behind him for a woman to feel his touch. Oh, and by the way, fat as he is, he's better looking than you, too."

"Lay off," Fat Guy said. "Just stop, Sammy. Boss wouldn't want you to—"

"Don't use my name," Old Guy said.

"Sammy? What a stupid name," Sy said. "Sounds like the name of a little kid, and I guess you have the intelligence of a six year old, though that might be underestimating your average six year old."

"Stop it!" Old Guy shouted, a break in his voice.

"You going to let that fat bastard tell you what to do, or aren't you a real man?" Sy continued.

Old Guy slapped her again, this time on her other cheek. His ring dug into her cheekbone. That was going to leave a mark.

She took one final breath before coughing in the direction of the old man and purposefully spitting in his face at the same time.

What happened next happened quickly, but she'd played it over in her mind so many times for the last few hours, it felt as though she was watching a movie she'd written herself.

She could sense Old Guy rearing back to strike her again, and, just as he swung, she let herself fall over. The old man's fist sailed past and, as she hit the floor, she heard Jorge leap up. Then she heard a scuffle.

She couldn't tell exactly what happened next, but she heard Old Guy howling in pain.

Scrunching her forehead and pushing the blindfold up with her shoulder, she managed to get it a fraction of an inch over her left eye, just enough to see. Jorge was on his knees, smashing the old guy's head into the floor with a rage as efficient as it was brutal.

Out of the corner of her eye, she saw Fat Guy fumbling for his gun. "Jorge!"

A second later, Jorge was yanking a gun from Old Guy's waist. *Pop pop.*

A quick double tap to the chest and Fat Guy fell heavily to the floor, gun still tucked into his belt.

Eyes scanning the room, still on high alert, Jorge panted. "Holy hell." He stood. "I did *not* think that would work."

"Me neither," Sy said.

Jorge found a shard of glass, rushed over to her, and cut the ropes binding her wrists.

Now free, Sy jumped up, adrenaline coursing through her veins. She felt for a pulse on the neck of the Old Guy, who lay bloody on the floor. He was dead.

Hurrying over to the dead man, she found his cellphone and held down the side button for five seconds, triggering an emergency call.

When 911 answered, she said, "This is Symone Aoki. I'm with Jorge Diaz Lopez. I believe you've been looking for him for a few days now. We're at a fish warehouse somewhere in Brooklyn. One captor dead, the other critical. Can you trace this call?"

CHAPTER FORTY

AUSTIN RACED through an alley and turned toward the beach. He hadn't been able to find a taxi, and now he'd been running for over a mile. He'd called the NYPD and even the mayor's office to tell them the location of the warehouse. He wasn't sure that's where Sy was being held, but he was willing to risk the embarrassment in case they could get there before him.

But they didn't.

At the end of the alley, the old warehouse loomed ominously. Rain soaked through his clothes and battered the weather-worn exterior, leaving rivulets of water to stream down its sides and pool in the cracks and crevices of the crumbling concrete.

A wind whipped off the Northern Atlantic, carrying with it the salty tang of sea and the faint, lingering scent of fish. It howled through the skeletal framework of the warehouse, moaning through the broken windows and adding an eerie soundtrack to the storm's cacophony.

Creeping around the side, he found an old busted window. He didn't see anyone. Didn't hear anything except his own breath and the heavy pitter-patter of rain.

Then he heard voices—quiet at first, then growing louder. He reached for his gun. Gripped it tightly.

The voices were headed straight for him. He crouched under the window, listening.

"This way." It was a man's voice.

Wait, was that Jorge's voice?

"We need to secure this area, in case anyone comes back." And that was Sy.

"Jorge?" Austin called, "Sy? That you? It's Austin."

Stepping back, Austin kicked open the old wooden door and ran into a brightly lit corner of the warehouse. Standing in the middle of the room were Sy and Jorge.

Sy's face was red and she had a small gash across her cheek, but she looked alright. Jorge looked much worse. His face was bruised and bloodied and he looked like he could barely stand. But he was alive.

Austin hurried up to Sy and hugged her, then pushed her away and inspected her. "You're alright," he said. "I'm sorry I left, I—"

"Hey," Jorge said, "what about me? I got the crap kicked out of me, too."

Austin smiled and hugged him as well. "Sorry. You look like hell, man. What's the status of this place?"

"Two goons down through there." Jorge pointed to an adjoining area. "Just finished a sweep and there's no one else here, but that could change."

"I called in this address," Austin said. "Police should be on their way."

As if on cue, lights flashed through the window.

Jorge set down the gun and took the phone from Sy. "I'm gonna call Maria."

Sy and Austin walked out together to explain the situation, then watched as the authorities swept the building.

"She's on her way," Jorge said, rejoining them.

"That's a relief," Austin said.

As they watched the officers securing sections of the warehouse one by one, Jorge explained how he'd managed to get the weapon off one of the two men who'd been holding them. He'd broken the man's neck, killing him instantly. The other man he'd shot in chest and he'd died soon after. Sy explained that another person had been there briefly as well, one she was fairly sure was The Magician, The Nightmare.

And as she spoke she had an odd look on her face, as though she was trying to remember something, a fact or name or number that was just out of reach, just on the edge of her mind.

An hour later, Jorge was across the parking lot sitting on the back of an ambulance and getting bandaged up as he gave his statement to a pair of detectives who stood under a large umbrella.

Austin was about to join him when the mayor and her staff arrived. Not wasting a moment, she approached Austin and Sy, who stood under a wooden entryway that faced the beach. "I should have your asses thrown in jail," the mayor began.

Austin got right back in her face. "You've got thugs in your financial district yanking innocents off the street and tossing them in vans, criminal warehouses sitting in plain sight, and you wouldn't even be here if I hadn't called it in. Half of me thinks you might be behind this entire operation. Because if you're not, you sure don't know how to run a police department."

Austin felt Sy's hand on his forearm. "Austin, she's *not* the one."

The mayor pushed Sy out of the way and stuck a finger in Austin's chest.

"Do you really think everything revolves around you, Thomas Austin?" Her voice dripped with disdain. "We've been investigating *The Magician* for over three months. We were close. And then you waltz in with your Western Washington cowboy antics and muddle up the entire operation." She paused for a moment, pinning him with a pointed look. "You've screwed up, Austin." Her laugh was sharp. A knife's edge. "You've interfered in an ongoing investigation and jeopardized months of hard work. I ought to throw *you* in jail." She leaned in, her gaze hard. "But I'll let you go on one condition. You drop this case and fly back to Washington immediately. No more meddling. No more rogue investigations. Just pack up your hero complex and go home."

"As for you, Ms. Aoki," the mayor turned her attention to Sy, her voice still laced with vitriol, "I'm sorry for what you went through. But you're not exempt from this either. As far as I understand, you're a suspended NCIS officer. Isn't that right?" She didn't wait for Sy to reply. "This isn't some sort of reality television show we're running here." The mayor shook her head, a sardonic smile playing on her lips. "This is New York City. We have laws, and we have order. We don't need renegade officers from out of state coming in and mucking up our investigations." She leaned back, crossing her arms. "Consider this your last warning."

Austin took in the verbal assault, watching out of the corner of his eye as Jorge's family arrived and ran to greet him. He pushed the medics aside to hug his wife, Maria, and his children. It was the kind of embrace that Austin liked best. The kind that told him that no one involved would ever take anything for granted again.

"Austin, are you even listening?" the mayor asked.

Austin took Sy's hand. "Not really," he said, leading her away from the mayor.

When they were out of earshot, Sy stopped him. "The Magician. He was there, in the warehouse. He asked me about you. I felt like I recognized his voice."

Austin watched her face contort in thought. She tilted her head and brought her hand to the back of her neck.

"No," she continued, "I think I imagined it. It was a guy. Definitely not the mayor, though."

"What did he sound like?"

"Male, somewhere in his thirties to fifties. Kind of a neutral accent but he could have been making his voice sound different. What makes you sure she won't arrest you? Arrest us?"

"Because we're the only ones who know how badly the city has screwed up this case."

PART 3

DIG TWO GRAVES

CHAPTER FORTY-ONE

WHEN AUSTIN CHECKED HIS PHONE, he had a new voicemail from the vet.

"Hello, Mr. Austin, we have good news. Run is going to be fine. Everything's calmed down over the last eight hours. We haven't left her side. Kendall is on her way over to take her home again. She'll need to take it easy for a few days, but we expect a one hundred percent recovery."

Austin shoved his phone into his pocket and stared out toward the beach, toward the Atlantic, and into the darkness. He wanted to get home and give Run a hug and let her lick him in the face for as long as she wanted.

As soon as he had that thought, his phone rang. Samantha.

"Hey," Austin said. "Thank you. I was able to find the location through your work. Turned out, my friends could take care of themselves, but, well, thank you."

"What happened?"

"I'll tell you all about it if I get home."

"*When* you get home," she corrected.

"Right."

Samantha cleared her throat. "I have something important to

tell you. It's what I was trying to tell you before. But now I know even more, and it's important. There is a New York-based Super PAC called *Justice Now*. It's been donating to both Daniels and Carter, Ridley's opponents. It's the one controlled by the billionaire, Talus Aaron Ockley."

"Okay," Austin said, "so what's new about that? Big, shady donations within politics is not exactly earth-shattering news."

Samantha sighed. "Let me finish. That organization brought me to a list of other big donor organizations, one of which is called *The American Leadership Committee*. About three months ago, they donated money to the mayor of New York City, who I know is one of the people you've been looking into. Then a month after that, she *returned* the donation, so I wanted to figure out why. Why would a politician give back money?"

"And?" Austin asked. "What did you find?"

"Well, I did a deep dive into *The American Leadership Committee* and it turns out it's a sub-organization of a larger company called *The Freedom First Coalition*." She paused, chuckling. "These guys really love their generic, patriotic, jargon-laced names. Anyway, at first, I figured it was just another big political organization funneling money to various candidates. Unethical, but not illegal. But that ain't it. *The Freedom First Coalition* is one of the ways the Namgung crime family funnels its money into both political clout and their own pockets. That's what they have been using to pay people off for years."

Austin considered this. "So, wait, why do you think the mayor returned the donation?" But as he asked the question, he had the answer. The mayor had just told him that she'd been looking into The Magician and the cartel for months. Most likely, she found out that they were connected and returned the donation to avoid any conflict of interest. "Is it possible the mayor received a donation from them and returned it when she found out who was really backing them?"

"That's what I was going to say," Samantha said. "*The Freedom*

First Coalition also gave many legit donations to politicians to cover their tracks. When you're corrupt, it's important to give money widely—both to implicate more people and also to not implicate the people you're funneling most of your money to."

"So let me get this straight," Austin said, walking out from under the entryway and into the rain. "*The American Leadership Committee* gets millions of dollars from *The Freedom First Coalition*, and uses that money to bribe politicians?"

"Right."

"And the *The Freedom First Coalition* is a wing of the Namgung crime family?"

"Correct."

"And *The Freedom First Coalition* is used to funnel money to family members, into legitimate businesses. Basically to launder millions of drug money dollars?"

"Indeed. Except it's not millions. It's more like hundreds of millions."

Austin stopped and turned back toward the warehouse, where Sy was now standing with Jorge and his family. "I don't suppose you can tell me who they are funneling most of their money to?"

"I can't tell for sure," Samantha said, "but a hell of a lot of it went to a Philippines-based LLC called Shamrock-Orchid Holdings."

Austin felt the rain soaking through his clothes. "You said Shamrock Orchid Holdings in the Philippines?"

He didn't wait for a reply—he had to talk with Sy, then he had to make the riskiest call of his life.

CHAPTER FORTY-TWO

THANKFULLY, Austin hadn't changed his shirt since leaving his in-laws. Reaching into his breast pocket, he pulled out the card the deputy mayor had stashed there a few days earlier. Dialing the number, he felt his hand shaking.

Then someone answered, "This is Deputy Mayor Sullivan's phone. Who is calling?"

"This is Thomas Austin, calling for the deputy mayor. May I speak with him, please?"

"Just a moment," the voice on the line said.

Across the parking lot, Austin saw the mayor, who'd just gotten out of a TV interview in front of the warehouse. Likely she was taking credit for bringing down a piece of the notorious Namgung crime family. She was eyeing him suspiciously. He was too far away for her to hear him, but he was paranoid, so he turned away from her and walked toward the beach.

He'd asked Sy to look into what sort of orchids were associated with the Philippines, and then to check to see if she could find any record of the shamrock icon Joey Green had described as appearing on the number ten cans containing his payouts. He'd also asked her to get in touch with Patch Kellerman and give her everything they'd uncovered. He didn't know if he'd live through the next hour and, if he didn't, he wanted everything they'd found to come out.

"Tommy Boy, what's up? I hear some pretty bad stuff is going down. Anything I can do to help?" the deputy mayor's voice came through the phone.

"Yeah, I had a run-in. It's not good. I think I have some news. I've been working on the case about Fiona, and I think, somehow, the mayor may be part of it. You told me not to trust her, and I think you were right. Is there any way we could get together just for a couple of minutes? I don't feel safe talking about it over the phone and I don't know who else to turn to. You are one of the only people in New York City I trust at this point."

There was a long silence on the phone, then Amelio said, "Absolutely. I'm on my way back to Manhattan from Peter Luger right now. Where can I pick you up?"

Fifteen minutes later, Austin stood outside of the deputy mayor's limousine as the driver patted him down.

He raised his arms, revealing the holstered MR1911. "By all means. Long as I get it back when I leave."

"Absolutely," the man said, taking the gun. "He's not comfortable with weapons, even when wielded by law enforcement. You know how he feels about gun control."

"Right," Austin said.

The driver tapped on the window and the door to the back of the limo swung open. Amelio Sullivan sat like a king, reclining with a scotch in one hand and a sleek iPhone in the other. He wore a dark blue suit and a gold watch that reflected the overhead lights.

Next to him on the seat was a little box marked with the logo

of the famous Brooklyn steakhouse: *Peter Luger, Established 1887.*
"Ribeye with béarnaise," Amelio said, "Would you like some? I
paired it with a Screaming Eagle cabernet, but, too bad for you,
we finished that at the restaurant."

"No," Austin said, "I'm on the black coffee diet at the
moment."

Amelio chuckled, then rolled up the divider between the
back seat area and the driver. "It's a soundproof barrier because I
have to make a lot of important calls for work back here." His
face grew concerned. "I'm sorry about having to have him pat
you down. I get death threats damn near every day, and, even
though she asked me to be her deputy, I've been worried about
McKinley for months now. I hope what you're saying is not true,
but I fear it is. Tell me what's up."

"Okay," Austin said. "Let me start from the beginning."

CHAPTER FORTY-THREE

AS THE LIMO weaved its way through Brooklyn in the heavy rain, Austin spent most of the next ten minutes telling the truth, making sure to insert a few believable lies as necessary.

He told Amelio about how Fiona had been investigating the Namgung crime family, how elements within the NYPD and FBI might have been involved in a cover-up.

He told the deputy mayor how he'd tracked down four names through his relentless research, with the help of now-deceased NYPD detective David Min Jun. He explained how he'd come to meet Jorge Diaz Lopez and learned that he was not in fact part of the crime, but had been trying to solve it with Fiona. He shared how he'd spent the last few days hunting for the truth, how he'd met Joey Green, and how he'd finally learned that Mayor McKinley had been the mastermind of the plot all along.

"She is known as *The Magician*," Austin concluded. "Some call her *The Nightmare*. From what I can tell, she has been receiving millions of dollars from the Namgung crime family—funneled through an organization called *The Freedom First Coalition*. She's used it to enrich herself and pay off members of the NYPD and FBI to allow the drug trade to flourish. Christopher Palini,

Gretchen Voohrees, and Jackson Baker. Those are three of them, but they may already be dead. And there may be others, too. When Fiona was close to bringing the mayor down, she had her killed. I still don't know who fired the shot, but I do know who gave the order."

Amelio blinked slowly and ran a hand across his bald head, as though taking it all in.

And that's when Austin knew he had him.

When he and Fiona had played cards with him years ago at the fallen officer benefit events, Amelio had been a heavy gambler. And Fiona had found his tell. Whenever he was about to bluff, he'd run a hand over his head and slow his blinking, almost as though he was concentrating hard to keep his story straight.

Amelio opened his mouth, but Austin interrupted him, holding up a single finger. "Hold on a second," he said, "I need to make a call." He dialed Sy and, when she picked up, he asked, "Did you find anything?"

"I sure did." Austin lowered the phone and put it on speakerphone so Amelio could hear. "As you know," Sy was saying, "the shamrock is often used as an icon of the Irish and Irish-Americans. The waling-waling orchid is one of the most important flowers in the Philippines. It was easy enough to pull up Joey Green's case file. The logo he described on those number ten cans looks a lot like a shamrock interwoven with waling-waling orchids. If you are where I think you are, you're in danger. But just tell me one thing, what does his cologne smell like?"

Austin inhaled deeply. "Spice, and maybe citrus."

"That's him," Sy said. "That's the man who was in the warehouse when I was tied up. Tell me where you are."

Amelio's hand moved to the cubby next to the rack of decanters on the limo's sidewall. When he pulled it back, he was pointing a Cabot Guns Black Diamond pistol at Austin's stomach.

He watched Amelio's eyes carefully. "Sy, you're going to want to look into a Philippines-based LLC called Shamrock-Orchid Holdings. It's the—"

Before Austin could finish, Amelio had grabbed his phone and tossed it across the car.

With a chilling calm, he then eased back into the plush leather seat. The dim interior light glinted off the cold, metallic surface of the gun he held casually, almost dismissively, in his lap. The weapon was not brandished with bravado, but rather rested in front of his stomach, the barrel subtly angling upward, his finger poised on the trigger.

Across from him, Austin sat still, his chest rising and falling with short, controlled breaths. "What now?"

CHAPTER FORTY-FOUR

AUSTIN STARED AT THE GUN, a stunning piece of lethal artistry. The Cabot Guns "Black Diamond" was crafted from a single piece of steel and boasted a sleek, obsidian finish. Its intricate detailing and diamond-checkered grips hinted at the weapon's extravagant price tag, while the compact design made it a deadly companion in the hands of the deputy mayor.

"How much did Fiona tell you about how things were between us when we dated?" He asked the question as though they were old friends catching up after a long time apart. The grin on his handsome face sickened Austin.

"Very little," Austin said.

"There was always something about her. Something I enjoyed. But I knew it was never going to work out between us because she was too, I don't know, *something*. Did you ever get that sense? That she was just too, *something?*"

"No," Austin said. "She was smart as hell. Smarter than either of us. But, Fiona wasn't *too* anything. She was perfect. For me, at least."

Amelio shook his head. "Well, she wasn't quite right for me."

"I know who you are," Austin said. "I know you are The

Magician. The Nightmare. Everything I said about Mayor McKinley applies to you. You pulled the strings. You've been the one all along. And *you* had Fiona killed."

Amelio smiled.

Of course, he wasn't just going to admit it. So Austin continued, "You know, Fiona once called you the 'one good politician.' And I believe you were good, at least at some point, long ago. My guess is that you started out bright-eyed, optimistic that you could fix things. You could make the city better, make people better, make yourself better, perhaps. But once you saw that things were pretty screwed up around here, once you saw how the first bit of corruption could sustain you, you were weak enough to decide you had to have your piece. And you took it. Then you kept taking, and taking, and taking."

Austin leaned back and rolled down the window, letting the rain hit his face. The night had grown colder and it felt as though tiny ice particles were barreling into his face. "I don't care what you do to me at this point," he said. "A friend of mine told me that when you set out for revenge, you should dig two graves. One for your transgressor. One for yourself." He turned back to Amelio. "Even if it's only one grave, and even if it's mine, it's okay. We've got you. Even if you kill me. We've got you. Buddy, your grave's already been dug." He looked away again and stared out at the buildings of Brooklyn as they approached the famous bridge that led into Lower Manhattan.

He knew what Sy would be doing at that moment. She'd be telling the mayor, the NYPD, and anyone else who would listen that Amelio Sullivan was The Magician. The Nightmare. The man behind the biggest case of corruption in New York City in years, maybe decades. The man who allowed endless drugs to pour into New York City from southeast Asia.

She'd be telling them that she'd smelled his cologne when she was being held captive, that he was behind an LLC called Shamrock-Orchid Holdings, which was the recipient of hundreds of millions of dollars of Namgung crime family drug money. She'd also be sharing all of this with Patch Kellerman, whom Austin trusted with the story only because breaking it would win her the fame she'd always desired.

It occurred to Austin that there was one more thing he needed to know. "The men who fired the bullets. What happened to them?"

Amelio said nothing.

"They shot me four times and I lived. They shot Fiona once and she died. But what happened to them?"

Austin heard sirens coming from behind. Perhaps Sy had acted even quicker than he expected.

Austin didn't think that Amelio would flee.

Men like him had other people do their killing for them and paid a lot of money for other people to fight their battles in court. After all, the evidence against him was all circumstantial at this point, and financial crimes were much harder to prove. Plus, Austin imagined, the money he had to defend himself would be virtually limitless. At the very least, he could stay out on bail for years as his lawyers used every tactic of delay in their arsenal. He believed they'd get him eventually, but the truth was, he wasn't certain.

So when the police car wedged in behind them, Austin assumed Amelio would ask the driver to pull over.

But he didn't.

Instead, he rapped on the window and shouted, "Get us out of the state, now."

CHAPTER FORTY-FIVE

AUSTIN WAS about to lunge for the gun, but he'd missed his chance. Just as fast as he had rapped on the divider and given the driver orders, Amelio had the gun trained back on Austin.

"Have you ever fired it?" Austin asked.

Amelio smiled. "You knew you were going to be my hostage."

"I thought it was likely," Austin said.

"What do they have on me?" Amelio asked.

Austin held his gaze. "They have everything."

"Everything? You're lying." Just as Austin had known Amelio's tell, Amelio knew Austin was bluffing.

The driver took a turn and eased onto the ramp for the Brooklyn Bridge. The police lights dimmed. They seemed to have been pulling over another car.

"We have Joey Green," Austin said. "We have two people kidnapped by your goons, one of them can identify you."

"They were blindfolded."

"I've got a kid named Michael. Maybe we can get him to flip on you. I'm sure we can."

"Never heard of him," Amelio said calmly.

"Kid has the cutest grandmother, maybe we can get her to

lean on him. Offer to fix her up in the finest memory care facility government money can buy."

This was one of the strangest conversations Austin had ever had, a rational back and forth about the evidence against a man whom he would prefer to see dead. It was as though Amelio wanted to weigh the evidence to figure out his next move.

The thing was, Amelio did not strike him as a bloodthirsty killer. He was something even worse.

He was a businessman who would do anything to win. Austin doubted he'd ever shot that gun. And Austin knew he was making a calculation. He was trying to decide what gave him the best odds. Unless there was overwhelming evidence against him, Amelio probably knew that his control over the city and the press had a chance to get him off. But part of him, Austin thought, also wanted to pull the trigger. Wanted revenge on Austin.

"It's like this," Austin said. "We have a lot. Joey Green. The shamrock and orchid on the cans. It represents your Irish and Filipino heritage, right? But more than that, we have a money trail. NYPD, FBI, they're running digital forensics right now connecting you to a web of corruption that will fill the papers for months."

Austin *hoped* that was true, just as he hoped they could eventually track down Michael, the young man who'd gotten his grandma all those parking tickets. But the truth was, he didn't know.

They were halfway across the Brooklyn Bridge, rain coming so hard now that it sounded almost like gunfire as it struck the roof of the car.

"Like I said," Austin repeated. "We have a lot. Enough. More than enough. Why do you think I was confident enough to get in this car without a gun? I knew I could convince you we had you and that killing me would only make things worse for you. You don't want a murder on your hands, too. You damn *coward*."

He spat the last word at him, unleashing years of anger and frustration and pain.

Amelio seemed to be considering Austin's words, and Austin knew he was about to get shot.

He saw the gleam in Amelio's eye as he pulled the trigger.

At the same moment, Austin dove to the right and grabbed the crystal decanter full of what he was sure was extremely expensive whiskey.

CHAPTER FORTY-SIX

THE BULLET GRAZED Austin's side, tearing his flesh but not causing any permanent damage as it lodged itself in the leather seat. Austin howled with pain but gripped the crystal decanter, swinging it at Amelio's face as hard as he could.

The man's jaw cracked, a sound as beautiful as it was sickening. A small amount of whiskey sloshed out through the built-in pour spout, its smell permeating the vehicle.

But Amelio didn't give up easily. He leaned back and aimed again, but in a second Austin lunged across the limo, grabbing at his wrists. He was able to disarm him, but, in their writhing, he got his foot stuck underneath the seat, leaving him vulnerable.

Amelio kicked his knee up and landed a blow in his chest, knocking him against a row of glasses secured to a small shelf.

Suddenly, the limo stopped. Horns blared everywhere. Traffic had halted behind a crash ahead.

Amelio opened the door and burst from the limousine. He took off at a full sprint down the blocked traffic lanes of the bridge.

Austin scrambled out after him and fell into a crouch, pulling the tiny taser from his boot, where it had been stashed all along.

At a sprint, he crunched over shattered glass as he passed the car crash. Amelio angled left, toward the edge of the bridge, and passed under a lamp. His face was streaked with blood, his eyes alight with malice.

Austin bolted, quickly closing the distance between them and following him along the railing. When he was ten feet away he fired the taser at Amelio's back, but the downpour was coming in at an angle, striking them despite the fact that there was a pedestrian walkway above them. The rain distorted his aim, the droplets colliding with the taser's probes. Instead of sinking into Amelio's back, they embedded themselves harmlessly into the rain-soaked pavement, sparks dancing off the wet surface.

The men collided on a narrow beam of iron in a flurry of fists and savagery. Amelio swung first, a wild miss that Austin sidestepped. Austin triggered the taser, pressing it up against Amelio's side.

Amelio jerked back hard and swiped down, knocking the taser out of Austin's hand.

Austin countered with a precise jab to Amelio's ribs, right where he'd connected with the taser. Their brawl inched closer to the edge, the churning East River 125 feet below. Amelio swung forward with a wild kick, but Austin dodged and followed with a knee to his gut, then a skull-rattling headbutt that knocked Amelio into the guardrails and down onto his knees and left Austin's ears ringing.

Half blind, Austin leaned over and snatched for Amelio, but his hands slipped off the man's bald head. Then he got hold of his mouth, fishhooking him by the cheek and smashing his face into the unforgiving iron girders that made up the bridge's railing.

Once, twice, three times—each impact echoed over the roar of the rain and the sound of sirens. "What happened to the men who fired the shots!" Austin demanded. "Where are they?"

Amelio looked up, his usual sneer gone for a moment. "Dead. Both of them. Everyone is dead. Except me."

Austin pulled Amelio forward by his collar. "How?" The word came out in a growl. Austin felt the reverberation of that question through his entire body.

"They were buried the day after the job. Clean up."

How could they be dead? How could everyone be dead?

He smashed Amelio's head into the girder again.

How could Fiona be dead in the first place? How had he ended up here?

Blood ran from Amelio's nose. Austin was so close to him that he could see the patterned imprint of the whiskey decanter on the man's cheek where he'd struck him.

Austin's thoughts cleared suddenly, and he looked down at Amelio's bloodied face, which still held a strange, sneering grin. Again, he smashed his head as hard as he could into the girder.

This time, he knew he'd hit his temple.

Amelio went limp temporarily, but then stiffened again.

He could taste his own blood and smell it too, as well as Amelio's blood and the icy rain. He could sense all of New York and the Brooklyn Bridge and all the history of the great and terrible city. His synesthesia kicked in, and he smelled and tasted something he couldn't describe and didn't understand. It was as though all the pain in all of history had taken hold inside him. All the tastes and smells at once and, somehow, he knew he was tasting suffering itself, death itself.

Austin tightened his grip on Amelio's lapel, pulling him back.

This would be the final blow.

He remembered Franklin, the homeless man who'd been screaming an unnamed anguish only days earlier. And now he knew why Franklin was screaming. He'd been screaming at the world for all the pain it offered, both earned and unearned.

He looked down at Amelio. This time, he let him go limp. He didn't see any sense in digging more graves.

For an instant, his focus wavered and he glanced back, distracted by a glint of light, a woman with a camera phone capturing it all.

Zzzzzzzz

Austin felt the shock bolt through his thigh and he jerked back.

Amelio had seized the split-second lapse to grab the taser.

Zzzzzzzz

Again he was tased, this time in the stomach. Austin heaved backwards, striking his head on the girder.

Amelio crouched, grabbing his legs. As he pushed Austin through the opening in the guardrail, the world tilted—bridge, sky, swirling river, Amelio's sneer.

Austin grasped at the girder, dangling, gripping. He slipped and fell further, but his bloody fingers clutched one of the steel cables, his feet dangling in the air.

Above, Amelio leered, his bloodied face contorting with savage excitement.

"Amelio Sullivan, freeze. Back away. Hands up!"

CHAPTER FORTY-SEVEN

A SERIES OF SHOUTS. Austin closed his eyes, gripping the cable with everything he had.

He heard footsteps. "Grab my hand." Austin opened his eyes. A burly officer in an NYPD blue uniform held out his hand. Another was spinning Amelio around to cuff him.

Austin braced himself, ready to reach out, but Amelio lunged forward, sliding like a baseball player skidding into second base. His designer shoes connected with Austin's fingers, breaking his grip.

Time seemed to stop.

The empty air beneath him seemed to go on forever.

Austin splayed out, head up, looking back up at the bridge as he fell.

The wind seemed to catch his back, moving him more upright. He thought of his parents and how they would feel when they heard the news. He also thought about Ridley, Jimmy, Lucy, Samantha, and everyone else back home. He even thought of Kendall. They'd had a rocky start, but he'd hoped for a better working future with her.

The officer who'd been trying to cuff Amelio fired a shot,

striking Amelio in the back. Amelio stumbled over the railing and Austin knew that, even though he was going to die, Amelio Sullivan would die seconds later, assuming the gunshot hadn't already killed him.

He almost smiled, then, watching Amelio's body following him down into the icy currents of the East River. And he felt like he'd done what he needed to do in this life to show Fiona that he loved her.

And then he thought of Run. Her sprinting down the beach like a cross between a rabbit and an overcaffeinated fox. Full of playfulness and enthusiasm and joy. He loved her more than he'd thought it possible to love an animal. And he wished he'd been more like her in life.

None of these were thoughts. Not really. They were simultaneous and instantaneous realizations that came as complete knowledge in the three seconds it took him to fall.

Then he closed his eyes and relaxed his whole body.

He'd done enough, and was ready to die.

CHAPTER FORTY-EIGHT

AUSTIN WOKE UP DISORIENTED. He blinked a few times, the bright light from above burning his eyes. It wasn't until he tried to move that he realized his leg was in a cast and his entire body ached in a way he never could have imagined possible.

He was in a hospital bed with one wrist handcuffed to the side rail. What the hell?

It was as though every part of his body had been individually beaten to a pulp and then taped back together by a drunk man. His skin, his muscles, his bones, even his toenails hurt. His right leg had clearly been broken and operated on while he was out.

But he realized he was alive. That was the biggest shock of all.

The last thing he remembered was falling. He was sure it would be the last thing he experienced. But it wasn't. He was still here.

He looked out the window. He was in the same Manhattan hospital he'd been in when he was shot. When Fiona was shot. The sky outside was gray and cloudy, and he could almost smell the fumes rising from the exhaust fans of the buildings surrounding them.

A nurse in bright pink scrubs walked in. "Mr. Austin, how are you feeling?"

"I..." Austin could barely speak. His lips hurt. His cheeks hurt. His eyes hurt. Everything hurt.

"As you probably figured out, your leg is broken and you're pretty badly bruised," she said. "Well, beyond bruised. But you ought to be dead. Only three people have ever survived a fall from the Brooklyn Bridge. If that storm hadn't been raging, you wouldn't currently have the honor of being the fourth."

"I don't... understand." Austin took a guarded breath and winced at the pain, then continued. "How am I not?"

"You should be," the nurse said. She picked up his hand and moved around the handcuff, which relieved some of the pressure on his wrist. "Any burning pain or tingling up your arm?"

"No."

"Ridiculous that we have to keep you cuffed. It's your legs that aren't gonna get you very far, Mr. Austin, and this handcuff here could cause you nerve damage if we don't get you range of motion exercises frequently enough. When a patient is under arrest, there's supposed to be an officer present to uncuff you for us when we need." She tisked audibly, then continued to assess the rest of his body, checking pulses then asking him to squeeze both of her hands before shining a flashlight into his eyes.

"How am I alive though?"

"Had to research about it myself." The nurse moved down to the end of the bed, pinching his toes and feeling for a pulse on the tops of his feet as she spoke. "Apparently, when the water is still, it's a harder surface to hit, less give. The fact that the waves were choppy decreased surface tension and kept you alive. Plus, you happened to hit feet first. Even with that luck, if that boat hadn't been going by, you would have drowned within minutes. Long story short," she pointed up at the ceiling, indicating where she thought heaven was, "someone up there doesn't want you dead. And I'm glad because the way you smashed that bastard's head against the bridge made me stand up and cheer. Always knew that guy was sketchy."

"What?"

"The video of you went viral. Your fight with Amelio Sullivan. Dude is deader than dead, but it's since come out that he was the ringleader of the biggest drug cartel in the city. Patch something or other... biggest story in years, although I just listened to the podcast version. Thanks for beating the crap out of him first. Selfishly, I don't want to take care of any more of his drug related casualties on my shift, do you know what I mean?"

Austin didn't know what to say.

"Push that pain button sweetie, no sense in suffering. Right now, you've got a lot of healing to do." She marked a few things off on a clipboard and tapped a few notes into an iPad, then pushed Austin's tray table towards him and walked away.

Austin felt around in his bed with his free hand until he found the end of an electric cord. He took the nurse's advice and pressed the button. *Thank god for patient controlled analgesia,* he thought as the pain numbed slightly.

His eyes closed and again everything went black.

The next voice Austin heard was Ridley's. "Damn, man, you look like absolute hell. I'm missing half a leg and I look better than you. I just went through a political campaign and haven't slept more than a couple hours in a month and I look better than you. You look like you went twelve rounds with the East River and lost. Badly."

Pain started in his stomach and rippled through his chest as Austin chuckled. He tried to open his eyes, but they seemed to be glued shut. Very slowly, he forced his mouth open and said, "What are you... doing here?"

Austin listened to Ridley's footsteps pacing the hospital

room. He wasn't sure if he was dreaming, but he didn't think so. He'd had little storms of dreams over the last, what was it? A day? An hour? He didn't know how long it had been since the nurse was there, but in his dreams he wasn't in so much pain. The pain reminded him this was real.

"I came to help," Ridley said. "Video of you smashing the deputy mayor's face into the Brooklyn Bridge went everywhere. Despite the fact that Sullivan was who he was, you can't just go vigilante and beat a dude to within an inch of his life."

"Self defense."

"I know, but you ended up in the hospital and you've been charged with attempted murder. Some hotshot prosecutor wants to make a point. The thing is, a day after you landed here, your friend Symone fed the biggest story of the year to Patch Kellerman. Then she followed up with *The New York Times*, *The Washington Post*, *Fox News*, *CNN*, the *BBC*, and anyone else in the world who would listen.

"Long and the short of it is, the story nails Amelio Sullivan. You and Sy nailed Amelio Sullivan. He's dead, but they've already grabbed about six lower-level people. More will follow, and it might even lead to some of the suppliers in southeast Asia. FBI is all over the money trail, too."

Austin felt tears welling in his eyes. He was glad he wasn't watching the news or seeing the newspapers. Glad to be in here so he could avoid reporters. But they'd done it. And if Austin had to spend the rest of his life in jail, he was fine with that.

"So why are... are you here?"

"Well, I'm the governor-elect of Washington State now and—"

"You won?"

"*We* won. Samantha had a lot to do with it. Lot of people did. But anyway, we do a lot of business with New York State. With New York City. I came to see if there was anything I could do to keep you out of jail. Mayor is gonna work on it, and

I think she can get everything dropped, given the circumstances."

"Thank you," Austin managed. "And congratulations."

"There's someone else who wants to see you as well. I'm going to go get a coffee and I'll be back in a bit."

Austin opened his eyes slowly and blinked into blurry light. A woman dressed all in white hovered over him. It was Sy, and she looked like an angel. "Maybe this is the morphine, or whatever narcotic they've got dripping into my system through that bag over there, but you look incredible." Austin patted the bed, encouraging her to sit. It hurt to hold his eyes open, so he let them fall closed. He could smell her hair, jasmine and citrus, and also her cappuccino.

Sy perched on the edge of the bed. "Let's not talk about anything that happened," she said. "Maybe sometime, but not now and not for a long time. I don't know about you, but I need a break. I need to do something I enjoy. I need to have some fun. I don't know when you're going to get out of this, but when you do, let's do something fun together."

Austin could hear the fatigue in her voice.

He reached out slowly and, fumbling, put his hand on hers. "Okay. When I get out of here we'll do something fun."

CHAPTER FORTY-NINE

Coney Island

Two weeks later

OLIVE HAD ALREADY RIDDEN the Wonder Wheel twice, and Austin watched as she ran back in line for a third go. Sy trailed a few yards behind, trying to keep up.

From where he sat in his wheelchair—his broken leg stretched out before him—he could see the joy radiating from her as she went round and round, her laughter echoing over the hum of the park.

She had spent the better part of the day exploring the park, her energy seemingly inexhaustible. She she'd tested her aim at the try-your-luck game stalls, throwing darts at balloons and knocking over milk bottles, and had won a stuffed bear nearly as big as her.

Austin chuckled as he remembered her devouring all but three bites of two Nathan's hot dogs, her face smeared with ketchup and mustard.

He'd promised Sy that he'd have some fun, and even though he had to sit out most of it, this was as close to fun as he'd come in a while. And at the same time, he was fulfilling the promise Fiona had made to bring her niece to Coney Island.

He'd only done one non-fun thing, and even that had been fairly satisfying. He'd read the story Patch Kellerman had written about the case and, even though he still wasn't fond of her, he had to admit she'd done a great job. She'd found out that Jackson Baker, Gretchen Voohrees and Christopher Palini were, indeed, dead. She'd done a long interview with Jorge in which he'd explained his role, Fiona's role, and even Austin's role in the investigation.

Patch had even gotten Joey Green on the record, describing his small role in the operation.

But—perhaps most importantly—she'd gotten hundreds of pages of files from Samantha and spent days tracing Amelio's financial corruption back a decade. Elements of the Namgung crime family were still at large, to be sure, but one of the heads had been cut off, and a thousand little snakes were now crawling back to their caves.

The only piece she'd left out of her story was the corruption of Talus Aaron Ockley. It made sense. After all, though Samantha had found evidence of staggering corruption, Ockley wasn't connected to the Namgungs or the corrupt elements in New York City that let them operate. Austin figured Samantha would leak the information online and send it to other journalists, but Austin doubted it would get much traction. Ockley controlled enough of the internet to suppress stories, and most journalists were terrified of crossing him. So as much as Austin would have liked to see him get his comeuppance, that would have to wait for another day.

His phone dinged and he saw that he had a new voicemail from a (212) area code. Manhattan.

Mr. Austin, this is Andrea from the mayor's office. You remember me, right? We're sincerely sorry about what transpired, and as you can deduce, there's been a fair bit of behind-the-scenes maneuvering. As you know, your friend Ridley is quite persuasive. We'd be honored if you would join us for a public appearance tomorrow afternoon, where we can acknowledge and commend your exemplary work. We're also extending an invitation for you to return to the NYPD. We understand there were complexities that led to your departure, but we believe those difficulties belong in the past. You obviously have the work of law enforcement in your blood otherwise we wouldn't be where we are today. New York is a safer place, thanks to you. To echo the mayor, 'That Austin is a hell of an investigator.'

We're offering you a position at the same rank you left, with a clear trajectory towards becoming the top detective in New York City, and potentially even the Chief of Police within a decade. The mayor wants to collaborate, Austin. To make you famous. TV appearances. Book deals. Everything. She believes you could do some genuine good here. Please, give me a call and consider our offer.

A few minutes later, Olive and Sy emerged from the roller coaster with windswept hair and wide grins.

"Sy promised she would get you to listen to some Taylor Swift," Olive said, smiling in a way that seemed genuine to Austin. Although he had to admit that, with kids these days, he couldn't tell when he was being mocked and when he wasn't.

"It's not like I'm an expert," Sy said. "But I am a big fan of the recent acoustic projects she did. Very singer-songwriter, and I like it."

This triggered a memory in Austin. In the early days of their marriage, Fiona had sometimes listened to a singer named Lady

Gaga. Austin didn't really know one singer from another, but Fiona had told him she was the hot new thing and then she'd gotten very popular.

There was one song Fiona loved most that said something about a little girl who kept her dolls in diamond boxes. Austin had heard Fiona singing it in the kitchen many times, never really understanding the lyrics.

But now he felt like he *did* know what it meant to keep your dolls in diamond boxes. Fiona's whole life, the way she looked, the way she acted, and her career, and everything about her was like a diamond box. Perfection. High class. Precision. Brilliance. But there were moments when Austin sensed the little girl inside, the little doll living inside the diamond box.

He saw it now in Olive. Beneath the snarky, 12-year-old girl exterior, there was an excitement, a curiosity, and a passion that had been there in Fiona too, under her diamond box exterior.

"I promise I'm going to listen," Austin said. "I'm going to be pretty immobile for a while so I'll have a lot of time to sit on the couch and listen to CDs."

"What the heck is a CD?" Olive asked. She put her hands on her hips and put on a pouty face. "Just kidding. Even *I* know what a CD is even though I would never personally listen to one." She turned back in the direction of the roller coaster. "I'm going to go again."

"I'm going to sit this one out," Sy said, sitting on the bench next to him.

"Ridley did it," Austin said. "I got the message a little while ago. The mayor needs to clean up the fact that her deputy was a murderer and drug kingpin and she's using me to make herself look good."

"I saw," Sy said. "There are already stories about how she empowered you to help bring down a few rogue elements of the NYPD. It's sick." She shook her head. "But I'm glad you're not going to jail."

They sat for a long time, Sy finally breaking the silence. "You seem good. Better."

"Leg is healing a little."

"No, I mean better than before, emotionally, or something."

Austin thought about this. "I guess I'm healing in more ways than one."

Sy turned toward him. "All of this has made me think about my husband and, you know, I don't think you ever really stop grieving the kind of loss we've faced. The pain never fully goes away. But even if the grief never disappears, you *do* keep living. You find new melodies to hum to, new flavors to savor. Maybe you buy a Taylor Swift CD and find a moment of joy. There are days when you realize that the weight on your chest has eased, if only just a little. Or perhaps it's just that time dulls the sharp sting of fresh wounds. I don't know if 'okay' is a destination I'll reach again. But being here with you, someone who has navigated the same waters, makes me believe in the possibility of a bearable existence. That we can find a purpose, a direction amid the storm."

Her black hair was being blown by the gentle breeze and, even though she wasn't looking at him, he felt like she was there for him.

"Maybe the best we can hope for," she continued, "is to traverse this path with someone who gets it. To find solace in our shared silences. We've both endured the darkest darkness and, for whatever reason, we're still here." She looked up at him. "You fell from the Brooklyn Bridge and you're only alive because the fall happened in the midst of a violent storm. I don't know what that means, but it means something."

Austin watched a few scattered leaves blow across the walkway.

"Anyway," Sy said. "I put in my papers. I'm leaving NCIS. And I wouldn't mind spending more time with you if you're up for it, and only when you're ready."

Austin looked at her. "As soon as I'm out of this wheelchair I'm flying back to Washington. Once I settle in a bit, get my bearings, you'll be the first person I call."

CHAPTER FIFTY

Seattle

Another two weeks later

AUSTIN LIMPED OFF THE PLANE, pausing in the tunnel leading to the terminal. He'd gotten out of his wheelchair the day before and he'd booked himself a ticket after walking his first fifteen feet in a month.

He took a deep breath. Though the temperature was no different than in New York, the air here had a unique scent. It must be the evergreens, he thought. Even within the concrete confines of the Seattle airport, their smell permeated the atmosphere.

Balancing a small carry-on in one hand and a cane in the other, he ambled slowly through the airport, pausing at a gift shop filled with smoked salmon, miniature carved totem poles, and oversized nightgown t-shirts still advertising *Sleepless in Seattle*.

He had no baggage to claim as he'd left everything but his

phone and wallet in the hotel room he'd abandoned back in Manhattan. He'd never see his trusty MR1911 again. It had disappeared in the chaos, but that was okay. Sy had helped him replace his phone while he was in the hospital. He was carrying a new ID, a couple hundred bucks, and that was it.

By the time he exited the building, the sun had set, painting the sky the color of a deep bruise. But it wasn't raining. And that made him happy.

On a whim, he decided to forgo the taxi, his original plan and the doctor's stern advice to minimize his walking. Instead, he found his way to the light rail. It would take him into downtown Seattle for just a few dollars.

The car was sparsely populated, a few lone souls scattered across the seats. He chose a spot near the back, settling in as the train began its rhythmic dance towards downtown Seattle.

The rail cut a path through the cities, offering glimpses of the industrial sprawl of Tukwila, a patchwork of warehouses and factories punctuated by the occasional fast-food joint. They passed stops for Rainier Beach, Columbia City, and Mount Baker, the buildings growing taller, the lights brighter, the pulse of the city stronger. Here, the grittiness of the suburbs gave way to the imposing shine of skyscrapers, their glass exteriors reflecting the city's neon heartbeat.

And when the downtown Seattle stadiums came fully into view, it struck Austin for the first time that he was truly almost home.

Austin emerged from the train station, and walked toward Pike Place a few blocks, before turning West toward the waterfront, stepping gingerly onto the steep hills that shot vertically down towards Alaskan Way. The biting chill of the evening air was a stark contrast to the warmth of the train carriage he'd left behind. He began his descent, his cane tapping a steady rhythm on the concrete. As he walked, the city unfolded around him in all its messy vibrancy.

He passed scattered groups of homeless people, huddled in doorways or alleyways, their meager possessions bundled around them.

Further along the streets, refuse littered the sidewalk, remnants of the day's activities discarded without thought. Yet, amid the grit, life was being lived. Young people, vibrant and full of energy, spilled out of bars and restaurants. Couples strolled hand in hand, returning from dinner or perhaps just beginning their night. The streets hummed with the roar of engines, luxurious vehicles purring alongside the grumbling of older, more dilapidated cars.

It was a chaotic symphony, and he was happy to hear it.

Austin sat on the top deck of the ferry, letting the cold wind tousle his hair. He stared off in the direction of Bainbridge Island as the bright lights of Seattle gradually receded behind him.

He'd told the mayor that he would consider her offer of returning to the NYPD. After all, being a detective was what he was made to do. But he knew now that his deliberation was over.

He was heading back to his forever home.

They could offer him the position of Chief of Police, unlimited wealth, anything in the world, but he wasn't going back to New York City. That chapter of his life was closed.

He'd begun realizing this the day after his trip to the amusement park when, for the first time since the funeral, he visited

Fiona's grave. He brought a simple bouquet of sunflowers and he went alone using a cabulance and a high end electric wheelchair the mayor had procured for him—a thank you and I forgive you. He stayed for hours, intending to ask her what she thought about the idea of him moving back to New York City, about finishing what they'd started there together.

But he hadn't asked her any of that.

Instead, he just sat quietly, sometimes smiling, sometimes crying as he said goodbye to the woman who sang along to the song about keeping her dolls in a diamond box.

His apartment was cold and quiet. He hadn't known when he would get home, so Run was spending the night with Kendall. He knew he'd missed her, but he didn't know exactly how much until he walked into the house without her there to greet him. But he'd see her tomorrow. Tonight, he had one more thing to do before he collapsed into bed.

He pulled out his phone and headed into the spare room, where Fiona's typewriter still sat unused on the desk. Finding the Washington State Police website, he downloaded the form to apply for a police academy exemption based on prior service. He pressed "print" on his phone and the printer hummed to life.

He was going to have his expired New York City Police license transferred to Washington State. When the form printed out, he put it into Fiona's typewriter and slowly, methodically, began entering his information.

He was going to apply to be a detective in the Kitsap County Sheriff's Department.

No sense in deferring his destiny any longer.

Early the next morning, Austin found himself sitting in the back of the little community church a few doors down from his general store, café, and bait shop. As usual, he'd let himself in through the side door.

For a couple of years now, he'd been going there because it was the only place Fiona felt present. Something about the smell of the place triggered his synesthesia and brought back memories of which he didn't know the origin. For whatever reason, his odd sensory cross-wiring brought her back whenever he was there.

But this morning, for the first time, she was gone.

The room was quiet and still, and the air held a neutral smell —perhaps a touch stuffy and dusty, with a hint of lavender cleaning solution.

But Fiona was not there.

Then it struck him that she'd *never* been there. The whole time, it had only been his need for her.

He'd been casting her into the present in a desperate attempt not to lose her. And now, for the first time, she was truly gone.

But the realization didn't come with pain.

It was only his need for her that had disappeared, his desperation.

He could still look back fondly, and he always would, but something had changed. He knew it would still be a long process, but for the first time, he felt like he might actually be able to move on.

Strolling across the street towards his little café, which was set to open in half an hour, he saw his number two man, Andy, heading through the back door.

Surely he was getting ready to make pancake batter, get the bacon going, chop potatoes, grate cheese, mince onions for the omelets, and do all the other things Austin loved doing himself but hadn't been doing much of lately.

He stopped in front of his store when he heard a car door slam.

Kendall was there, looking much more relaxed than the last few times he'd seen her, and wearing her trademark black leather jacket.

She looked around the parking lot. Seeing no moving vehicles, she opened the back door of her car and said, "Let's see who's here."

Run jumped down into the lot. She sniffed the air in all directions, spotted him, and let out a single, exuberant bark. Then she bolted towards Austin at a speed that reminded him of the first day he'd brought her home.

Austin smiled as he sat down in an Adirondack chair in front of his store, his busted leg stretched out in front of him, his arms open as wide as they would go.

—The End—

Thanks for reading! If you're enjoying the series, check out Thomas Austin Book 8: *The Silence at Mystery Bay*.

A NOTE FROM THE AUTHOR

Thomas Austin and I have three things in common. First, we both live in a small beach town not far from Seattle. Second, we both like to cook. And third, we both spend more time than we should talking to our corgis.

If you enjoyed *The Nightmare at Manhattan Beach,* I encourage you to check out the whole series of Thomas Austin novels online. Each book can be read as a standalone, although relationships and situations develop from book to book, so they will be more enjoyable if read in order.

If you enjoy pictures of corgis, the beautiful Pacific Northwest beaches, or the famous Point No Point lighthouse, consider joining my VIP Readers Club. When you join, you'll receive no spam and you'll be the first to hear about free and discounted eBooks, author events, and new releases.

Thanks for reading!

D.D. Black

ALSO BY D.D. BLACK

The Thomas Austin Crime Thrillers

ABOUT D.D. BLACK

D.D. Black is the author of the Thomas Austin Crime Thrillers and other Pacific Northwest crime novels that are on their way. When he's not writing, he can be found strolling the beaches of the Pacific Northwest, cooking dinner for his wife and son, or throwing a ball for his corgi over and over and over. Find out more at ddblackauthor.com, or on the sites below.

facebook.com/ddblackauthor

instagram.com/ddblackauthor

tiktok.com/@d.d.black

amazon.com/D-D-Black/e/B0B6H2XTTP

bookbub.com/profile/d-d-black